Abigail

RUNAWAY BRIDES OF THE WEST · BOOK 15

BEST-SELLING & AWARD-WINNING AUTHOR

NANCY FRASER

This is a work of fiction. Names, characters, places and incidents are either the product of the author's imagination or are used fictitiously, and any resemblance to actual persons living or dead, business establishments, events, or locales, is entirely coincidental.

Abigail
Runaway Brides of the West – Book 15

COPYRIGHT © 2022 by Nancy Fraser

All rights reserved. No part of this book may be used or reproduced in any manner whatsoever without written permission of the author except in the case of brief quotation embodied in critical articles or reviews.

Books From a Romantic's Heart Publishing
Contact Information:
romwriter96(at)gmail(dot)com

Cover by Black Widow Designs © 2022

Chapter One

Bartlesfield, Texas
Early Summer, 1870

Abigail

Abigail Willoughby counted the money she had accumulated in secret over the past ten days. Thirty-six dollars and eighty cents. Not much, especially given the task she was about to undertake. If her father knew what she was planning, he would surely lock her away in her room and throw away the key.

At least until the following Saturday.

That was the day she was to wed Simon Champion, the owner of the adjacent cattle ranch, and her father's new business partner. Together, Joseph Willoughby and Simon Champion were going to become the largest producers of beef cattle in not only the state of Texas, but also the entire country. And, all it had taken to secure the merger was the promise of Abigail's hand in marriage.

Her father was ecstatic at the possibility of their

union. No doubt he thought she was too far on the shelf for anyone to want her. Truth be told, she still wasn't certain why Simon had asked for her hand at all. Especially when they barely knew one another except for polite conversation during his frequent visits to the ranch.

Given she was twenty-six and never married, it wasn't as if she had a gaggle of men eager to court her. Yet, her lack of eligible suitors hadn't mattered. She had her art, and that was all she'd ever really needed. Yet now, with her future—a future she'd not asked for—all mapped out for her, Abigail found she needed one more thing.

To escape.

As quickly, and as completely, as possible.

A light tapping sounded at her bedroom door causing Abigail to quickly slide the bills and coins into her dressing table drawer.

"Yes?" she called out.

Jewell, her father's housekeeper, opened the door a crack and asked, "Is there anything else, Miss, before I leave for the day?"

"No thank you, Miss Jewell. I have everything I need."

"Maggie left a few of her almond cookies in a tin on top of the icebox if you get hungry later."

Abigail spared a brief thought for Maggie's

talent in the kitchen. Having her meals prepared for her was definitely something Abigail was going to miss. Especially given she, herself, didn't know how to cook.

"Thank you. I will likely have one with tea before I retire for the night." As an afterthought, she asked, "Did my father say how long he'd be gone when he left earlier?"

Jewell cleared her throat, as if weighing the discretion of her words. "He's gone to see Missus Beecher, so he'll likely be there a while."

Madeline Beecher was her father's latest paramour. Widowed nearly as long as Abigail's father, the woman made no bones about the fact she'd be more than happy to snag herself another rich husband. Given the sizable estate the late Mister Beecher left behind, Abigail couldn't understand why the woman would want to be bothered finding another husband.

With her father out for the evening, and the household staff gone as well, Abigail moved freely around the large home. She carefully packed a medium-sized carpetbag with the very barest of necessities and stored it in the downstairs cupboard. Given the route she'd planned wouldn't allow for much, she chose her three plainest dresses, one fancier outfit, a sparse assortment of undergarments, an extra pair of shoes, a lightweight coat, and—most importantly—her sketchbook and pencils.

Her canvases, fine horsehair brushes, and pots and pots of paints would have to be forfeited. Perhaps, once she was settled and able to secure herself a position of some sort, she could replace all she was leaving behind.

At precisely quarter-to-six the next morning, Abigail hitched her roan mare to the smallest of her father's buggies for the drive into town. Given how late her father had arrived home last evening, he would likely sleep until the staff began arriving at eight. That gave Abigail an hour's head start on the seven o'clock stage. Her travel route was intricate and depended on the help of one friend here in town, and an artist friend she had met just last year.

The horse and buggy ready, she retrieved her carpet bag from the cupboard and made her way toward town. Sara, her closest friend, would take the horse and buggy to the livery once Abigail was safely away.

Abigail's heart filled with sadness at the thought of all she was giving up to escape marriage to a man she didn't love. A man who only sought her hand to seal a business deal. Surely such a beginning wouldn't bode well for a lifetime commitment.

"Thank goodness you've arrived," Sara said when Abigail pulled into the dooryard of Sara's small home. "I thought perhaps you'd been discovered."

"No, I… well… I had a moment or two of indecision. This is such a big move, but one I'm determined to make."

"Have you decided on a final destination yet?" Sara asked.

Abigail shook her head. "I'm thinking of going to Saint Louis."

"So far? I know you want to put distance between you and your father, but the longer you spend traveling the greater the risk of being found."

"I'll get as far north as Fort Worth, and then make my decision," Abigail explained. "From Fort Worth, I can go north, east or west."

"Once you're settled, you'll write to me, won't you?"

"Of course. I will let you know where I'm at, as long as you promise to not tell my father."

"I promise," Sara assured her. "Now, let's get you on that stage before someone in town sees you leaving."

Abigail checked the brooch watch clasped to the jacket of her traveling suit and adjusted the fit of the heavy bonnet she'd donned to hide her reddish-blonde hair. She was the only passenger at the moment, but likely more would board at the next stop. They'd been on the road for over an hour, and she felt as if she could sit back and relax.

There had been no one she knew anywhere near the stage depot before they left. Thankfully, even the station itself wasn't open for the first run of the day, so she was able to pay her passage directly to the driver.

As far as she could tell, nobody from hometown—other than Sara—knew she was gone. Now, if she could make it as far as Fort Worth without detection, she should be successful in her escape.

The dry dirt road was unforgiving, sending a shock of pain up her back each time the wheel hit a rut or a bump. When the driver stopped for twenty minutes at the Prattville station, three people boarded. Among them was a middle-aged couple, and a rather suspect looking man in dark clothes who chose to sit on her side of the coach, but as far away as he could get.

A fact for which Abigail was very grateful.

"So, my dear, I'm Grace and this here's my husband, George Parker. We're on our way to Fort Worth to see our newest grandbaby. We have five now." She drew a breath, then asked. "What's your name, and where are you headed all alone?"

"My name is… um.. Elizabeth. Elizabeth Grant. I'm meeting a traveling companion in Fort Worth," Abigail fibbed. "And then, hopefully, we'll be able to secure rail passage to Saint Louis." She *was* meeting her artist friend, but they wouldn't be traveling together, so Abigail reasoned she told a half-truth—all done in order to obfuscate her true objective, as well as her identity.

"It's a shame the way the railroad fell into ruin after the war," Mister Parker commented. "It's coming back now though, thanks to the hard work of those Germans fellas who settled here in the past few years."

"Yes," Grace agreed. "They're hard workers to be sure. We hired one gentleman to care for our small farm while we're away."

"How about you, fella?" George asked, his question aimed at their companion.

"Heading to Oklahoma, I reckon," the man said. "Just looking to get out of Texas."

Abigail wondered if the man was running from the law. He had the look of a gunslinger, all dark and brooding, with a gun belt strapped around his hips. Immediately, she stroked 'going east' off her travel plans.

They stopped for the night at a waystation to give both the passengers and the horses time to rest. Abigail paid her four-bits, and then took the key to her single room from the man at the front counter. "The facilities?" she asked.

"Out back. Women's privy is to the right, men's is to the left."

Abigail stifled an outright gasp. "No indoor plumbing?"

"No, missy, this ain't the big city. Be grateful we change the sheets on your cot once a week."

She spared a fleeting thought for her huge four-poster bed and comfy feather mattress. Yet, beggars—or runaways—couldn't be choosy, she supposed. Eleven hours had passed since they'd left Bartlesfield. By now, her father was aware of her absence, rather than just assuming she had gone into town to shop.

Abigail wasn't worried that he might come for her himself. It would take more than her leaving to get him away from his ranch and other business interests. Unless, of course, her leaving soured the entire deal with Mister Champion.

Hopefully, the two men could come to some other arrangement. After all, it wasn't as if she were such a valuable prize that it would cost her father his coveted merger.

"Come on, girlie. The stage ain't going to wait for you to get all gussied up," the coach driver hollered. "Bad enough you insisted on taking your bag inside with you last night. Now I gotta load it up top again."

"I'll help her."

Abigail raised her head and met the dark stare of the stranger she'd deemed an outlaw.

"Thank you, sir," she said, handing off her carpetbag. "We never did get your name."

"That's 'cause I didn't give it," he responded. "You can call me Jesse."

"Jesse," she repeated. "I appreciate your help."

He doffed his worn black hat before climbing up the spokes of the wheel to secure her bag on the roof of the stage. By the time he jumped back down, she and the Parkers were already seated in the coach.

"How long until we reach Fort Worth?" Grace asked the driver when he came to lift the ladder and shut the door.

"We should be there by mid-day, assuming we don't run into any trouble."

"What kind of trouble?" Abigail asked.

"Broken wheels, or robbers. Highwaymen travel these roads all the time," the driver explained. "Lucky for us, I got a rifle and I'm a right good shot."

Somewhat absently it seemed, Jesse ran his hand over the six-shooter strapped to his hip. As it has done the day before, her imagination reeled with possibilities. Was Jesse a highwayman set to rob them? Or, perhaps, he was on the run from an untenable situation, same as her.

They arrived in Fort Worth at half-past two. Abigail was never so grateful to be off her backside and standing in an upright position.

"For those of you going on," the station master announced, "the ticket window will be open for another three hours. There's one more stage in about an hour heading east. There are rooms to let for the night not far from here, and wagons to take you to the train station if that's where you're going. Tomorrow morning, there are stages going west at six-thirty and eight in the morning. You'll need to get your tickets for those today, since the station doesn't open until eight-thirty."

Abigail said her goodbyes to Grace and George, watching intently as they climbed into a carriage driven by a handsome young man who she guessed to be their son-in-law. Jesse, she noticed, had gone inside to purchase his ticket east and find himself something to eat.

She was about to follow the station master

inside to inquire about where the westbound stages were headed, when a familiar voice called out her name.

"Abigail Willoughby, is that you?"

Abigail turned and lifted her fingertips to her lips to request her friend Carolyn's silence. Closing the short distance between them, she whispered, "As far as anyone knows, I'm Elizabeth Grant."

"Oh, right. I forgot." Tugging on Abigail's arm, Carolyn coaxed. "Follow me. My carriage is over here. We'll get your bag loaded and then go to the café for lunch."

"I wanted to ask about destinations going west, if you don't mind waiting."

Carolyn withdrew a piece of paper from her pocket and waved it in the air. "I've got the schedule right here. We can look it over while we eat, and then we'll do as we planned, with me buying the ticket so nobody's the wiser about where you're going."

"I mentioned to my traveling companions that I was meeting a friend and we were possibly taking a train to Saint Louis. I'm hoping that will be the information that gets back to my father."

"I'll do my part to uphold your ruse," Carolyn assured her. "It's the least I can do for someone who taught me how to properly mix colors of paint."

Chapter Two

Bent River Ranch
Cripple Creek, Colorado

Randall (aka Rand)

Rand McIver opened the gate leading to the far pasture and coaxed the twenty head of cattle out onto the open range. Rain fell in sheets, drenching him clear through to the bone. Twenty feet away, his tethered gelding whinnied his displeasure in being subjected to the unseasonably chilly weather.

"Get over yourself, you spoiled animal," Rand grumbled. "If I gotta be out in this mess, then so do you."

Not for the first time in the past few days, he admonished himself for giving his ranch hand a week off to travel to Denver for his daughter's wedding. The fact his housekeeper had up and quit on him just the day before also added to his frustration.

Housekeepers—good ones at least—were hard to

find, especially in this remote town twenty miles south of Colorado Springs. Finding a replacement was likely going to be a fool's errand. Still, he had to try.

"Come on, Bolt, let's head back to the barn," Rand coaxed. "I've got a feed of oats waiting for you, and a pot of coffee sitting on the stove for me."

While he drank his thick-as-mud coffee, and silently cursed Missus Carroll for quitting, Rand wrote out a 'help wanted' notice to place on the board at the mercantile. As an afterthought, he wrote up two more copies—one for the café and another for the livery. Not that he expected to find a housekeeper boarding a horse, or having one shod.

He'd wait for the rain to stop and then saddle Bolt a second time for the ride into town.

"Afternoon Rand," Cyrus McCready called out. "What can I get for you today?" Hoisting a tin up in the air, he added, "I got a new item in today. Tinned milk of all things. Some lady named Borden back east invented it. Stays fresh until you open it."

"I don't have much use for milk," Rand admitted. "It's not like I'll be doing much cooking other than beans and whatever meat's hanging in the smokehouse."

"I heard Eugenie up and quit on 'ya. Word is

she's moving east to live with her sister. I guess since Bert passed, she's lonely here on her own."

"She had me and Malcolm," Rand pointed out. "I always figured she liked nagging on us for things."

Cyrus snorted a laugh, nearly choking on the wad of tobacco stuck in his cheek. "Yea, that's every woman's dream to spend her days taking care of a couple ornery cowboys."

"I was hoping I could hang a notice on your board. I need to find a new housekeeper, preferably one who can cook as good as Eugenie."

"What you need is a wife. And, I don't just mean for cookin' and cleanin'."

"I got enough trouble fixing up Bent River after my uncle nearly let it go to ruin. I don't need a woman telling me what's what."

"Your uncle was a fine man, a great preacher, but not much of a rancher. When one of his parishioners left him that place years ago, he should have sold it and built himself a place closer to his church. That was where his heart was, not on some plot of land."

"I was surprised he kept it, too, but I guess he figured I'd need a place to live when I got back—assuming I didn't get myself killed during the territorial disputes."

"I'm betting he knew you'd make something of

the place if'n you got the chance." Nodding toward the far wall, Cyrus told him, "Go ahead and put up your notice. I'll keep an eye out as well."

"Just don't go sending me some woman who's only looking to get hitched," Rand warned. "I have no time for courting."

"Got it. You want a middle-aged woman, married or widowed, who can cook and clean."

"Yep. In the meantime, though, I'll take some canned beans and maybe a tin of that fancy milk for my morning oatmeal."

Rand dropped off the second notice at Brewster's Livery before stopping in to see his friend, Bill Winkle, the town's sheriff.

"Hey, Bill," Rand greeted when he went through the jailhouse door. "I was heading over to the café for a bite to eat and thought I'd see if you wanted to grab your supper at the same time."

"Sorry, Rand, but Sadie made me a box lunch. You're welcome to stick around and share it with me. She always packs more than I can eat."

"Nah, you go ahead and enjoy your meal. I've got to drop off a for-hire notice, so I'll get myself something at Myrtle's."

"Eugenie's gonna be hard to replace," Bill commented. "You know what you need—"

Rand raised his hand, stopping Bill's words in

their tracks. "Yes, I know. I need a wife. Like I told Cyrus less than an hour ago, it isn't going to happen. So, all you happily hitched fellas can just stop bugging me about it."

"A woman that doesn't leave at the end of the day might be a blessing, especially when winter gets here."

He purposely shot his friend a dark glare. "I got myself some wooly long underwear. I'll be just fine."

"You know, there is another option," Bill offered. "You could get yourself a mail-order bride. No courting required."

"Um... no thanks. If I were in the market—and I'm not—I'd at least want a gander at the goods first."

Bill's smirk was loud enough to be heard all the way to Colorado Springs. "I'd reckon the woman would feel the same way about getting a look at your ugly mug, too."

Rand threw a wave over his shoulder as he exited the jailhouse and led his horse to the post outside Myrtle's Kitchen Café.

"Evening, Miss Myrtle," he greeted as he stepped inside. "What's good tonight?'

"Hello, Rand. Everything's good, but the roast beef dinner is my specialty. Comes with potatoes, mashed turnip, and a slice of cornbread. If you want dessert, it's apple pie and costs an additional ten cents."

"Sounds good, pie and all." When Myrtle dropped off his plate and cup of steaming hot coffee, he asked, "I wrote out an advertisement for a new housekeeper. Any chance I can tack it up by your front counter?"

"I suppose. Not like there's a lot to choose from around here though. If they're coming in here to eat, they might not be the best cook."

"You're probably right about that," he said, chuckling. "However, it doesn't hurt to try."

Abigail

Five in the morning came far too early for Abigail, especially since she'd not slept a wink on the horribly lumpy mattress.

Are you sure it was the mattress and not your fear of the unknown?

If she were being honest with herself, it was probably a bit of both. In hindsight, she should have accepted Carolyn's offer to stay with her at her boarding house, yet she'd not wanted to leave any trace of her arrival in Fort Worth, so she'd taken a room at the hotel under her assumed name.

She could hear the front desk clerk going from door-to-door giving a sound knock to wake up the travelers in time to make the six o'clock stage. After reviewing the schedule with Carolyn the day before, Abigail had decided on a small town about twenty miles south of Colorado Springs. Somewhere she wasn't likely to be found. As planned, Carolyn went to the station and bought the ticket. As an added precaution, Carolyn made sure her coal-black hair was visible beneath a lightweight summer bonnet.

Now, as she dressed, Abigail chose darker colors and a full bonnet.

The stage ride would take four days to get from Fort Worth to Colorado Springs. Four days to wonder if she'd made the wrong decision, four days to keep looking over her shoulder, four days that would eat up even more of her meager finances.

You should have gone to the bank back home before you left.

Yet, she hadn't for fear the manager would alert her father to an unusual withdrawal and possibly tip her hand.

"Good morning, Miss," the stage driver said when she arrived at the station platform. "You heading to Colorado Springs?"

"Yes, sir." Digging into the pocket of her skirt,

she pulled out her hand, and told him, "Here's my ticket."

"Just one bag?"

"Yes, sir."

"The name's Hank. No need to call me 'sir.'"

When Hank offered her a hand into the coach, Abigail placed her fingers in his and smiled. "Thank you... Hank."

The moment Abigail took her seat, the young man to her right gave a tip of his hat, and said, "Hello, I'm Andrew Carlson. Nodding to the man across from him, he added, "This here is Mister Wilber Newton, and next to him is Miss Arabella Smith."

"Nice to meet you all," Abigail responded. "My name is Elizabeth Grant."

"What takes you to Colorado Springs?" Mister Newton asked.

"I'm visiting a friend who lives on the outskirts of town," she responded. "How about the rest of you?"

"I'm on my way to Denver to take over as the bank manager for my current employer," Mister Carlson explained.

Miss Smith fidgeted a bit in her seat, but then said, "I'm also heading to Denver to get hitched."

"Congratulations, Miss Smith," Abigail told her.

Turning to Mister Newton, she asked, "How about you, Mister Newton? Why are you going to Colorado Springs?"

"I'm returning home. I live about halfway between Colorado Springs and Denver, and was only here on business."

"What business is that, sir?" Andrew asked.

"I'm a cattle broker."

Abigail drew in what she hoped was a silent breath. No doubt a cattle broker would know of her father and Mister Champion. She made a mental note to be careful what she said around the older man.

"Listen up, everyone," Hank announced before closing the door. "We've got four days and three nights on the road. We only stop overnight one time, so you might want to get used to sleeping sitting up. Other than the one night, we'll be stopping only long enough to swap out the horses, driver, shotgun rider, and for food and privy breaks."

Another man came to stand beside the stage. Peeking his head in through one of the windows, he said, "My name is Horace." Hoisting up his hand, he added, "This here's one of my three rifles. It's my job to protect you on the first leg of this trip. When we stop, don't go wandering off any farther than the outhouses."

"If'n you're all ready," Hank told them, "We'll be getting underway."

The stage lumbered along the main road until they reached the edge of town. The moment they were clear of the last building, Hank snapped the reins and the team of horses picked up speed.

"It's going to be a long ride," Wilber confirmed. "Perhaps you ladies would be more comfortable sleeping in shifts. That way one of you can sit with Mister Carlson and me, and the other can stretch out on the opposite seat and sleep for a spell."

"I'm perfectly fine sleeping sitting up," Miss Smith said. "Unless Miss Grant here needs some room to rest."

Abigail shook her head. "I'm fine with the arrangements as they are, but thank you for the suggestion, Mister Newton."

By the end of the second day of travel, Abigail wished she'd not been so hasty to choose seated sleep. Every muscle in her body ached and her backside was surely bruised from all the bumping around.

Hank and Horace had left them that morning, replaced by two rather foul-smelling men who'd not bothered to introduce themselves. Thankfully, tonight was the layover, and they could all get a good rest. With any luck, the driver and guard would take a bath when they stopped.

It was mid-day on Friday when the stage pulled into Colorado Springs. Once the driver dropped her bag on the wooden platform, he climbed back onto the stage and drove away, her three traveling companions now on their way north. Most suddenly, Abigail felt very alone.

Picking up her belongings, she walked into the waystation and up to the desk.

"Hello?" she called out when there was no one at the counter.

"Be right there," a man responded. He came through the curtained-off doorway a moment later and asked, "How can I help you, Miss?"

"I've just arrived on the stage from Fort Worth. I'm on my way to a town called Cripple Creek. When is the next stage going that way?'

"At four-thirty, so you got an hour to get yourself something to eat, and freshen up. You can store your bag behind the counter if you want."

Abigail hefted the bag up and handed it to the clerk. "Thank you. Where can I get a sandwich and cup of tea?"

"There's a dining room in the hotel next door. Or, there's Millie's Diner about halfway down the road and on the other side next to the sheriff's office."

"The hotel dining room sounds fine."

"What's a young lady like you doing going to Cripple Creek? Ain't much there but a couple of mines and a few rundown old farms."

"I have friends," she said simply.

"You're not one of those fancy mail-order brides, are you?"

A soft laugh escaped before she could rein it in. "No, not me. I'm just visiting."

Or, more precisely, I'm hiding out.

Chapter Three

Cripple Creek, Colorado

Abigail

The station master in Colorado Springs wasn't joshing when he said Cripple Creek wasn't much to look at. As the stage rolled slowly into town, Abigail spotted a livery, a dimly lit saloon, the mercantile, a café, and a boarding house. The driver drew to a halt in front of the jail where the sheriff waited to greet anyone who might choose to disembark.

While this might not be exactly what she had in mind—one thing was for sure—nobody was likely to come looking for her. With that realization in mind, another thought came to her. Would there be work for her here in such a small community?

She was educated so she could teach. Assuming, of course, there wasn't already a schoolmarm in place. Or, even children to be taught.

"Hey, Bill," the driver shouted when he jumped down to the ground. "Just got one to unload."

The sheriff opened the door of the coach, and Abigail stepped through, cautiously accepting his offered hand.

"Welcome to Cripple Creek, Miss."

"Thank you. I assume by that star on your chest, you're the sheriff."

"That I am. Bill Winkle is the name. And, you are?"

Abigail hesitated. Should she continue to use her abridged name, or take a chance on properly identifying herself?

"Abigail... Abigail Grant," she said finally, clinging to at least part of her assumed name.

"Well, Miss Grant, what brings you to our little town?"

When the driver tossed down her carpetbag, Sheriff Winkle caught it in one hand and offered her his opposite arm. Abigail felt she had no choice but to accept.

"I've been looking for a quiet place to settle down," she told him. "After my mother passed away back in Saint Louis, I wanted to get away from the city."

"So, you're planning a permanent move?"

"Assuming I can find work and a place to live."

"There's not much of either around here, I'm afraid. The boarding house is men only, and there are no jobs that I know of… um… one maybe."

"Doing what?" she asked, fearful it might be something untoward at the saloon.

"A local rancher is looking for a housekeeper and cook. The lady working for him moved back east to live with her sister."

"Is he an honest and God-fearing man?"

"Randall McIver is as honest as the day is long. Although, his faith has been tested one too many times to call him a true believer."

"Would I be required to live there, with Mister McIver? Alone?"

"That's something you'll have to work out with Rand. Eugenie lived here in town with a friend and the woman's husband and drove her buggy back and forth every day."

"How far is it?"

"His place is about twenty miles outside of town, but easy to get to. I'm sure he has a spare buggy you can use. However, the difficult part will be finding an available place for you to live."

"Do you think he might hire me?"

Bill Winkle raised and lowered his dark gaze, taking in her length but not in an awkward or uncomfortable way.

"You seem fit enough. As long as you can cook and clean, I see no reason why he'd not at least give you a chance."

Abigail wrestled with yet another half-truth. About the only thing she knew how to cook was her father's favorite spicy chili, and her housekeeping skills were limited to caring for her bedroom and art studio back at her father's home.

Still? How hard could it be?

"Is there somewhere I can hire a horse and buggy?" she asked. "I'd like to meet with him today if it's not too late."

"I was just closing up for the day," the sheriff told her. "I reckon I can give you a ride out. We can stop at my place along the way and I'll ask my wife if we can put you up if necessary, at least until you and Rand can settle on arrangements."

"I appreciate your kindness, sheriff. I truly do."

"Don't go getting too grateful until we see if things are going to work out."

Rand

"Dang it!" Rand muttered, dropping the hot skillet on top of the wood-burning stove and shoving his burned fingers beneath the water pump at that sink. One pump, two. By the third full lift and fall of the handle, cool water flowed freely over his aching hand. He was about to wrap a tea towel around his injury when the sound of a wagon rolling into his yard drew him to the back door.

Bill Winkle's spotted mare trotted into view, followed by the buggy usually reserved for Bill's wife Sadie. A woman—who was not Bill's wife—sat beside him on the front bench.

Rand couldn't get a close look at the woman, her face obscured by the brim of her bonnet. Could this woman possibly be here to apply for the open housekeeping position? He couldn't think of another reason for Bill to arrive unannounced, and shortly before supper time.

Stepping out onto the porch, Rand nodded his head in Bill's direction. "This is a surprise, Bill. I wasn't expecting you." Turning to face the woman at Bill's side, Rand added, "Or, anyone else for that matter."

Bill stepped down onto the dirt and offered the woman his hand. It irked Rand that he still couldn't get a good look at her. She'd lowered her head, her attention drawn to the ground at her feet.

"This here's Miss Abigail Grant, and she's lookin' for work," Bill told him. "She's also in need of a place to stay. However, if that's not something the two of you are comfortable with, Sadie says we can put her up for week or so." Leading the woman forward, Bill added, "Miss Grant, this is the fella I told you about… Rand McIver."

"Evening Miss Grant," Rand said, his greeting causing her to lift her head and meet his gaze. Her clothing was dark. Not mourning dark, but a rusty shade of brown. The bonnet covered her head entirely from forehead to the top of her jacket collar.

"Good evening, Mister McIver," she responded. The unique sound of her voice—a strange mix of warm honey and strong whiskey—made his insides flip.

"Come on in," Rand suggested. "I was about to make myself some supper, but that can wait until we talk. There's coffee on the stove, if you'd like some."

Bill snorted a laugh. "No thanks, Rand. I've had your coffee." Taking Abigail Grant's elbow to escort her up the stairs, Bill clarified, "Rand's coffee is strong enough to choke a rattler, assuming one would be dumb enough to take a sip."

"I have tea, if either of you would prefer," Rand offered.

"Tea would be nice, if it's not too much trouble," Miss Grant said.

"I'll grab myself a glass of your cold well water," Bill said. "Best in the county."

Once Rand poured tea leaves into one of his late uncle's porcelain cups and filled it with boiling water, he set it in front of his guest.

Miss Grant wrapped her hands around the steaming mug and pulled it closer, before saying, "It's awfully warm in here. Do you mind if I remove my coat and bonnet?"

"Suit yourself," Rand responded.

The moment she removed her heavy traveling coat, Rand realized how small she was. Short and thin, and not at all what he had in mind for a housekeeper. No doubt if they stood side-by-side, she'd barely reach his collarbone. He took a closer look at her hands. They were delicate. Not the hands of a woman used to manual work like tending a home, washing dishes, or weeding a garden.

This isn't going to do at all.

By the look on Bill's face, he'd likely come to the same conclusion.

Rand was about to say as much when she reached up and released the ribbon holding the bonnet close to her throat. With a single brush of her fingers, she pushed the heavy covering aside. Long, red hair, shot with strands of gold, fell like rays of sunlight across her shoulders. Bill nearly choked on his mouthful of water.

Rand's gut tightened. Abigail Grant was beautiful, her features as dainty as her size.

But not suitable for your needs.

Silently, he cursed at his inner voice.

"So, Miss Grant, what experience do you have keeping a house and cooking?" Rand asked.

Her slim shoulders lifted and fell on a sigh. "After my mother's passing, I was in charge of our family home."

Rand shifted in his seat, trying his darndest to get a read on the woman. "Have you ever worked on a ranch?"

"We lived on a ranch," she said simply.

"In Saint Louis?" Bill questioned.

"I didn't say we lived in Saint Louis, sheriff, only that my mother died there."

Rand stood and walked to the stove to refill his coffee cup. He needed a moment to think. There was something not right about what she was saying yet, for some reason he couldn't quite fathom, it didn't seem to matter. "When can you start... on a trial basis, of course?"

"In the morning, assuming I can arrange a ride back from the sheriff's house."

Rand shot Bill a glance, not the least bit surprised to see his friend fighting back a grin. "No need to travel, if you don't want to," Rand said. "I've got a cabin out back between here and the barn you can use. It hasn't been lived in for a while, but it shouldn't take much to clean it up."

"That would be fine, assuming there won't be a problem with the people in town. I intend to join the church we passed on the way here, and I wouldn't want the congregation thinking I'm a loose woman."

"You're a Christian woman, then?" Rand asked.

"Yes. Is that a problem?"

He shook his head. "Not for me, as long as you don't expect me to take you there every Sunday."

"All I require is the use of a horse and buggy. I can get there myself."

Bill's smirk spread across his face, the reaction not lost on Rand.

"Why don't I leave you two to work out the details?" Bill suggested. "I'll grab your things out of the buggy and drop them on the porch." Raising his head, he met Rand's stare. "Perhaps, until you get the cabin in shape, you could sleep out there and let the lady have the house."

"I don't want to inconvenience anyone," she told them.

"Bill's right," Rand admitted. "There's likely spiders, maybe even a garter snake or two. You can sleep downstairs in my late uncle's room. I'll sleep in the bunkhouse until we get things in shape."

Once Bill had dropped off the traveling bag and left for home, Rand went back to the stove. He'd not eaten, and likely neither had his new, and no doubt inexperienced, housekeeper.

"Are beans and pork belly okay for supper?" he asked.

She nodded, sending waves of her silky hair sliding over her shoulders to land in the middle of her chest. Suddenly, Rand wished he'd asked Bill to stay for supper as well.

"I can get that on the stove, if you'd like," she told him.

"That's okay. I'll take care of it. No doubt, you've had a long day on the road. Tomorrow morning is soon enough to begin working."

Once they'd finished their meal, and worked together to wash the dishes, Rand carried Miss Grant's traveling bag to the back bedroom. She followed behind at a discreet distance, yet he couldn't help but inhale the scent of her rosewater cologne.

For a man who said he didn't need a woman, you certainly folded faster than a greenhorn with a bad poker hand.

"There's indoor plumbing," he told her, motioning toward the water closet opposite the bedroom door. "I wasn't expecting a guest, so I didn't light the outside boiler, so the water will be lukewarm, or possibly cold."

"That's fine," she told him. "I just need to wash

the dust off my hands and face."

"Is there anything I can get you before I head on out to the bunkhouse?"

"Do you work this place alone?" she asked. "Or do you have ranch hands?"

"I got one fella at the moment—Malcolm Tigley—but he's away at his daughter's wedding in Denver. He'll be back on Tuesday. I usually hire a few more men during branding season and when we move the cattle to the far pasture."

"How many head do you have?"

He was surprised by her question. Perhaps she knew more about ranching than he first believed. "A hundred and ten, three of which are due to calve over the next month. I'm still trying to get this place built up, so I'll add more when I can."

"I'd love to see the entire spread one day when we both have the time."

Rand gave a quick nod of understanding, then told her, "It's pretty spaced out and some places are only accessible by horseback." When she shot him a coy smile, he asked, "Do you ride?"

"Oh, yes. Ever since I was five."

"Well then, I guess I'll have to make some time to show you around."

There it was again, the twitch in his gut. The nagging feeling he'd made the biggest—yet most exciting—mistake of his life.

Chapter Four

Abigail

Abigail awoke with a start, the sound of someone moving around not far from her door causing her to bolt upright in bed. It took a moment to acclimate herself, but she finally realized where she was... in a stranger's home and about to embark on a new life based on a whole bushel of half-truths.

Hopefully, the Almighty would forgive her for what she had to do to escape her father's heartless business deal.

A tap sounded lightly on the wood frame, followed by Rand McIver's deep voice.

"It's half past. I'm going out to gather some eggs for breakfast. I brought a slab of bacon in from the smokehouse, if you want to slice some off and get it started in the fry pan."

Half past what?

Pushing her hair from her face, Abigail reached for her brooch on the side table.

Five? Half past five? Was the man crazy?

She might have grown up on a ranch but—other than during her recent travels—she rarely awoke before seven-thirty.

Well, your life is different now, isn't it?

Abigail swiped a hand across her face, pushing away the remnants of sleep from her eyes, then sat up on the edge of the bed. Yes, her life was different now, and she would have to learn to make the best of it. She'd just not expected her new life to start so early in the morning.

Dressed in one of her simple flower-print dresses, her long hair tied back with a sturdy ribbon, Abigail made her way to the kitchen. Coffee was brewing on the stove, its pungent aroma filling her senses. A kettle was also set over an open spot on the stove. The tin of tea leaves from last night sat alongside a clean cup and spoon on the nearby counter.

Her gaze was drawn immediately to the large slab of meat that lay beside the sink. Tingles invaded her fingertips at the thought of having to slice off hunks of raw bacon to cook. Her insides churned. She wasn't prepared for this. Perhaps she should ask Mister McIver for a ride back to town so she could look for another position. Or, possibly move on to a larger town where she could find work in a field more suited to her abilities.

You wanted anonymity. Believe me, no one will expect you to be hiding out in Cripple Creek and working as a housekeeper.

Sucking in a breath and holding it tight, she picked up the heavy knife and pulled the slab of bacon toward her. She would not let this hunk of dead pig defeat her.

"That was a decent breakfast," Rand said, hiding what she suspected was a laugh behind the rim of his coffee cup. "The cuts of bacon were a bit uneven, but I suppose that could have been the knife. I'll sharpen it on my whetstone before supper."

"The eggs were delicious, and fresh," she commented.

"They were still warm under the hen's feathers when I gathered them."

"How many chickens... um... hens do you have?"

"Eight layers. I'll take you out to the coop later and introduce you. Most are docile, other than Henrietta."

"Henrietta?" Abigail repeated, amused by the idea that a grown man actually named his chickens.

"She's my best layer, but can be a bit cantankerous about giving up her bounty."

"I suppose we should discuss exactly what's expected of me as your housekeeper," she suggested. "I wouldn't want to overstep, or not do something I should."

"When it's just me and Malcolm, there's no need for fancy meals. Just meat, potatoes, and a vegetable. Maybe a pie for dessert."

"A pie?" she repeated, an annoying squeak invading her voice.

"Or, if you're more partial, a cake or bread pudding. There should be a loaf of stale bread in the larder." He reached across the table for the coffee pot and refilled his cup. "I suppose today would also be a good day to bake bread."

Abigail's throat went dry and she swallowed hard. "To tell the truth, I don't eat desserts—other than the occasional cookie—so I've not made a lot of them. And, I haven't baked bread in ages."

His square jaw twitched, drawing her gaze to the most interesting pair of lips she'd ever seen on a man. Narrow, bent slightly, with a scar that ran from just beneath his nose to the top left corner of his mouth. His chin had a cleft, and his cheekbones were high for a man. All in all, Rand McIver was a handsome fellow. Assuming you were someone who noticed those things.

"I figure dusting the house, making the beds, sweeping and mopping every day will be enough. Then, of course, the meals. The garden's in need of weeding, so you might want to get to that this afternoon while you're gathering herbs for supper."

Abigail felt faint. *How in heck's half acre would she accomplish all he was asking of her each and every day.* She should have been honest with Sheriff Winkle and admitted her skills were more suited to education or art.

"It'll take me a few days to get into a routine," she said finally. "But I'm sure I'll be up to snuff in no time."

"I've not got a lot to do today. Maybe I can give you a hand," he offered. "I'll take the weeding and herb gathering off your plate. I'll even bring in some fresh carrots and turnips for supper." When she met his gaze, he added, "I usually take my afternoon meal around noon. Something simple."

"Simple?"

"Eugenie used to make a spicy tamale casserole that was quite filling." Nodding toward the far cabinet, he told her, "She left her book of recipes on the shelf, if you want to look through it sometime."

"That would be most helpful," she admitted. "That way I know what kind of foods you like."

Rand downed the last dregs of his coffee and set the cup on the table next to the empty pot. Pushing himself to his feet, he made his way toward the door. "I'm going out to the barn to dust off the small carriage and check the tack. If you're planning on going to services on Sunday, I don't want you breaking down along the way."

"I appreciate that," she responded.

He cracked the door open but, rather than go through, he stopped suddenly and turned. "The cleaning supplies, broom and mop are in the closet at the end of the hall. I'll light the pilot under the boiler on my way to the barn. You should have mop water within the hour."

Rand

Rand wasn't exactly sure what Abigail was playing at, but he felt fairly confident in his assessment that she knew very little about housework, and even less about cooking. Yet, last night, after he'd hunkered down in the bunkhouse, she was all he could think about. Her smokey voice set his nerves on edge, made his gut clench. Even now, his pulse raced at the memory of her removing her bonnet to let those waves of reddish-gold silk fall freely across her shoulders.

Get your mind back on work, or you'll be useless for the entire day. And restless, the entire night.

He laid down the wood and lit the fire beneath

the huge boiler, as he'd said he would. Then, he made his way to the garden. There wasn't as much weeding as he'd let on, and he was done in less than a half-hour. After choosing a handful of herbs, he made one more stop, then slipped inside through the kitchen door as quietly as he could.

Abigail was somewhere down the hall. He could hear the soft lilt of her voice as she hummed one of his uncle's favorite hymns while she worked. The song brought back memories of his youth... memories he'd buried long ago during the injustice of the Colorado territorial skirmishes.

The things he'd seen, done, were not for the faint of heart, and definitely not Christian. For that reason, among one or two others, he preferred to spend his Sunday on the ranch, among the fields, and trees, and God's innocent creatures, rather than giving praise in the clapboard church Daniel McIver had built.

Rand set the herbs on the drainboard next to the sink, then took down a tall glass and filled it with water and the flowers he'd picked alongside the house, placing the bouquet in the center of the table.

He made his way to the door, intending to sneak out, when he was stopped short by Abigail's arrival. She'd put an apron over her dress and covered her hair with a bandana, yet little wisps stuck out and tickled her cheeks, drawing his stare.

"I've finished upstairs, other than the mopping," she told him. "I'm still waiting on the water to heat. In the meantime, I thought I'd start a pot of chili for lunch if you could either show me the way to the smokehouse, or bring in a few pieces of beef and pork. I put beans on to soak earlier."

"You make chili?"

She planted her hands on her narrow hips and shot him a teasing glare. "Yes. I make chili. I assume you like spicy food since you mentioned the tamale pie."

"I can handle spicy food, as long as you can."

The corners of Abigail's full lips lifted in another perfectly coy smile. "Then, chili it is."

Rand left to retrieve the requested meat from the smokehouse. He was barely a few feet from the open window when Abigail began humming again, another old hymn. Another long-forgotten memory.

"That was darn near the best chili I've ever eaten," Rand admitted before taking a long pull on his third glass of water.

"The cornbread was a bit dry," Abigail lamented. "I used Missus Carroll's recipe, but I think I left it in the oven too long."

Rand shrugged. "I ate it all, didn't I? Dipping it

in the chili helped."

"Yes, to your credit, you did finish everything I put on the table."

"Can I ask you a question?"

She met his gaze and nodded slightly. "I suppose, as long as it's not too personal."

"Have you ever worked as a housekeeper before?"

"Is it that obvious that I don't know what I'm doing?"

"A little bit. However, I do give you credit for trying."

"Are you firing me, after only one day?"

He shook his head. "No, I'm not. I figure if you're willing to try something you've never done before, you must be desperate for work. I'm desperate for someone to keep things up while I work the ranch, so I'm just as willing to make it work, if you are."

"Thank you. I appreciate the chance."

"Just answer one more question."

Her warm brown gaze flared slightly. "Which is?"

"Are you running from the law?"

"No, nothing like that. I promise."

"Well then, I see no reason why you can't stay."

Chapter Five

Two Weeks Later

Abigail

"Abigail?"

Abigail shifted in the chair in front of the parlor window, surprised to hear Rand's voice when he was supposed to be riding out to the north pasture.

"I'm in the parlor," she called back.

Rand appeared at the doorway seconds later, a huge grin on his face. "Beula's about to calve. You said you wanted to watch."

Abigail set aside her sketch pad and pencils and shot to her feet. "Yes, I do!"

"I can't believe you were raised on a ranch and never witnessed the birthing process."

"What can I say? My father thought it wasn't something a young lady should be a part of if she wasn't one of the ranch hands." She paused for a moment to study the man standing on the threshold of the room she'd claimed as her makeshift studio. "I thought you were going out to open the pasture gate."

"I was, but Malcom snagged me just as I was about to leave to tell me the birth was imminent."

"Just let me put on those fancy boots you bought me, and I'll be right there."

"You might want to change into your riding britches too. It can get a mite messy," he suggested.

Abigail nodded. "You go ahead, in case Malcolm needs your help. I'll be there in ten minutes or less."

She made her way to her bedroom and stripped out of her dress, discarding it on the end of the bed. Digging through the dresser drawers, she pulled out her riding trousers, and one of Rand's old plaid shirts from when he was younger. Smaller.

The past two weeks had been wonderful. They'd gone riding nearly every day, Rand proudly showing off the improvements he was making to Bent River Ranch.

Malcolm had returned on time and quickly took her under his wing. He was one of the funniest, kindest men she'd ever met, and patient when it came to teaching her the finer aspects of gardening.

While she was still learning how to properly clean a house as big as this one, Rand had taken over the mopping duties, claiming the water bucket was too heavy for her to tote around from room-to-room.

He'd also taught her how to make biscuits. Thankfully. Her first two efforts had been a disaster. And, he'd continued to sleep in the bunkhouse, rather than repair the cottage for her use. He was the consummate gentleman. Whether she wanted him to be, or not. Just the memory of laying awake at night, and thinking about the handsome rancher, sent a racing to her pulse.

However, now was not the time to think about how Rand made her feel. Now was the time for a new calf. She rushed from the bedroom, buttoning up her shirt as she went. Her boots were sitting by the back door and she slid into them on the run.

"You okay over there, little bit?" Malcolm asked, his mustache twitching in time with his words. "If'n it gets too much for you, just look away."

"I'm fine," she said, swallowing back the bile rising in her throat. "You weren't kidding when you said it was messy," she told Rand.

"Be grateful it's an easy delivery," Malcolm added. "Sometimes we have to stick our hand inside and yank the calf out."

Abigail turned away, retching, and threatening to upchuck her morning eggs and toast.

"Let it out if you have to," Rand said, chuckling. Before she could respond, he announced, "Here we go, almost out you little dickens."

"Well look at that," Malcolm exclaimed. "We got us a heifer."

Abigail turned back, her gaze taking in the small animal lying on the floor at her mother's feet. "She's... um... beautiful."

Malcolm's hearty laugh echoed through the barn. "She will be once we get her cleaned up a bit."

Little more than an hour later, the three of them were on their way back to the farmhouse for lunch when they were stopped short by Bill Winkle's arrival.

"Good day, sheriff," Malcolm hollered. "What brings you out of your office on this fine day?"

Bill climbed down from his horse and tied the reins to the nearby fencepost. "I need to talk to Miss Abigail for a few minutes."

An ache settled in the pit of her stomach. *Had her father discovered her whereabouts? Was he on his way to take her back to Texas?*

"I'll head on back to the barn and check on the mother and baby," Malcolm suggested.

"Is this a private conversation?" Rand asked, his gaze moving from Bill to her and back again.

"That's up to Abigail," Bill confirmed.

"It's okay if Rand sits in," she responded. "Whatever it is, I'm sure it'll be something he'll need to know eventually."

Once Malcolm had wandered off, Rand motioned them all into the house.

"What is it, sheriff?" Abigail asked when they'd each taken a seat at the kitchen table.

"There's a couple of things but, first and foremost, is a claim from a man in Texas that his daughter, Abigail Willoughby, has gone missing on the eve of her impending wedding. The marshal service in Fort Worth sent out notices to local law enforcement in the larger towns. The notice was forwarded to me by the sheriff in Colorado Springs who believes the woman may have come our way." Narrowing his gaze in her direction, he asked, "Would you know anything about that, Miss *Grant*?"

She drew a full breath and nodded. "Yes. I'm Abigail Willoughby. I chose to go by my mother's family name, Grant, in hopes it would help me go undetected."

"Breaking a marriage contract is a serious offense," Bill pointed out.

"There was no contract," she stated firmly. "Marrying me off to the owner of the neighboring ranch was my father's way of merging the two spreads. I never agreed to the wedding. And, given I'm an adult, he had no legal right to give me away to a man I don't love. Or, even respect."

"Exactly how old are you, Miss Willoughby?" Bill asked.

"I'm twenty-six, educated, and fully capable of deciding who and when I'll marry."

"While I agree with you wholeheartedly, I do have to do my duty and advise your father's solicitor that you've been located. Whether or not they desire to press the matter further is up to them."

"Surely, they can't force Abigail to go back to Texas. As she said, she's an adult and did not agree to the marriage," Rand reiterated.

"I'm no lawyer, so I don't know if a contract between her father and his neighbor is binding, given Miss Abigail did not agree," Bill explained. "Worse case scenario, she may need to go back to Texas and fight this in court."

"So, basically, as a woman, I have no recourse but to bow to a man's bidding," she responded sourly. Before either Rand or Bill could respond, she asked, "What was the other issue you wanted to discuss? You said there were a couple of things."

Bill huffed out a deep sigh. "There's been talk."

"Talk?" Rand repeated. "About what?"

"About Miss Abigail living here in your home. Some aren't buying the 'he's sleeping in the bunkhouse' story. That, combined with the fact she has no real link to the community, will only strengthen the possibility she may have to go back to Texas."

"*This* is her home now," Rand bit out. "And those old gossips in town can mind their own business."

Abigail considered all the trouble she'd caused, all the gossip she'd heaped on Rand, and suggested, "Perhaps, it would be best if I just went back." Shooting Rand a look, she teased, "I know that means you'll be out a top notch housekeeper, but at least you won't be the subject of the town's imaginings."

Rand stood quickly, the force of his movement nearly knocking over the chair. "Give me a second to think on this," he mumbled before storming out of the room.

Turning to Bill, she asked, "Where's he going?"

"Danged if I know."

A few minutes passed before Rand returned. He came to a stop beside her chair and, in a single fluid motion, dropped to one knee, and asked, "Abigail Gr... um... Willoughby, will you marry me?" He opened his clenched palm to reveal an antique gold and ruby ring.

"I... um..." she stuttered. "But why? I mean... you don't have to do this."

"Yes, I do."

"It would solve both your problems," Bill pointed out. "It would stop the rumors going around town, and you can't very well be expected to return to Texas to marry if you're already married."

"It also gives you part ownership in property, which gives you standing in the state," Rand added. "Given all the injustice I've seen, I won't let some antiquated laws, or another man's greed, force you into doing something you don't want to do."

She licked her suddenly dry lips and met Rand's intense gaze. "It's such a big step. For both of us."

"It is," Rand agreed. "However, I'd like to think choosing me is the lesser of two evils."

Abigail reached out and cradled Rand's lightly-stubbled cheek in her hand. "There's no evil in you, Rand McIver."

His grimace surprised her.

"It doesn't have to be a real marriage, if you don't want it to be. Or, at least, not until you're ready."

A flush rose in Bill's cheeks and he pushed himself to stand. "I think I'd better let you two talk this part over privately. Just send word when you make up your mind. I'll hold off on sending a response until I hear from you."

He'd about reached the door, when Abigail called out, "Wait, sheriff. You're right, we can sort out the finer details later, in private, but I can make my decision before you go."

She turned back to Rand. "Rand McIver, I accept your proposal of marriage."

His grin a mile wide, Rand slipped the ring on her finger and raised her hand to his mouth, pressing a gentle kiss to her fingertips. Their gazes met over the tops of her fingers, and she returned his smile with one of her own.

Across the room, Bill coughed discreetly. "Now that you've accepted, I can arrange for the county judge to perform the ceremony as early as next week."

"No," Rand responded. "I'm sure Abigail would prefer to be married in a church and, despite my reluctance to attend services, I'm willing to have the reverend perform the ceremony. The sooner, the better."

"You're right, I would like to be married in the church, but—"

"No 'buts' about it," Rand interrupted. "I'll ride on over to Reverend Dale's house and make the arrangements."

"Once the certificate is signed," Bill put in, "I'll send off a telegram to the state marshal's office explaining that I found Miss Willoughby but that she's now Missus McIvor."

"Does that fancy lawyer from California still have an office in Delphi?" Rand asked.

"To the best of knowledge, he's still in business," Bill confirmed.

"Where's Delphi?" Abigail wondered.

"Next town over," Bill explained. "Another hour or so on the stage and you'd have been there."

Abigail glanced around the room, her gaze scanning the warm kitchen and the two men across from her. "What? And miss out on this wonderful employment opportunity?"

Chapter Six

Cripple Creek Community Church
The Following Saturday

Rand

Rand stood at the front of the church, shifting nervously from one foot to the other.

"Stop fidgeting," Bill ordered. "You look like a cow about to be led to slaughter." Giving Rand a poke for good measure, Bill added, "If you get the urge to run, I tethered a horse at the side door."

"I'm not going anywhere," Rand insisted. "I'm just wondering what's taking so long."

Bill chuckled. "You'll get used to it. Women, especially those getting gussied up for a special occasion, can take forever."

As near as he could figure, the organist was about to run out of hymns to play. The small crowd that had gathered to witness the ceremony were squirming in their seats, the oppressive heat of mid-day making the men tug at their shirt collars, and the women fan themselves with the brims of their discarded bonnets.

"You don't think she ran again, do you?" Bill teased.

"I hope not," Rand whispered back. "You don't think she would, do you?"

"No, I don't. For two people who claim to be getting hitched for convenience, I've never seen—"

Whatever Bill was about to say was interrupted by the opening of the church doors. Bill's wife, Sadie, stepped through first, dressed in her finest Sunday outfit, a bouquet of wildflowers clutched in her grasp. At Rand's side, Bill straightened his shoulders, his chest puffing with pride at the sight of his wife.

"Does it ever get old?" Rand asked quietly.

"What?"

"The way you feel when you look at the woman you love."

"Not as far as I can tell."

Once Sadie had reached the halfway point of the long aisle, Abigail stepped through the door, her arm tucked firmly in the crook of Malcolm's elbow, a grin as big as the entire state of Colorado painted on his weathered face.

Rand's breath caught in his chest. The small crowd rose to their feet.

Dressed in a light violet dress, her long hair hanging loosely across her shoulders and topped with a ring of fresh flowers, Abigail was the most stunning woman he'd ever seen. He noticed the slight tremor of her hands where she held her bouquet made up of lily of the valley and dainty purple flowers, and wondered if her nerves were as jangled as his.

"You've got the ring, right?"

Bill rolled his eyes, but then nodded.

When Abigail reached the front of the church, Rand held out his hand and closed his fingers around hers. Together, they turned to face Reverend Dale. *This was it. They were getting married.* His heart clenched and then relaxed. *Why did something he'd avoided for so long seem so right?*

The minister motioned for everyone to sit. "Dearly beloved, we're gathered here today…"

Abigail

"By the power vested in me by God and the territory of Colorado, I now pronounce you man and wife."

The minister's words echoed in Abigail's head. She met Rand's warm smile, and welcomed the tightening of his grip against her trembling hands.

"You may now kiss your bride."

Oh… my! She raised her head, her attention homing in on Rand's mouth. His half-smile.

Leaning forward, he touched his lips to hers. The soft caress drew her sigh, and his low moan. Much to her surprise, he repeated the kiss with a bit more enthusiasm, the longer, warmer joining drawing a handful of guffaws from the men in the pews.

"That was nice, Missus McIvor," Rand whispered against her mouth.

"Yes, it was, Mister McIvor," she returned quietly.

Rand spun them both around to face the congregation before leading her down the aisle. Outside the church, they waited to accept congratulations from those in attendance.

"There's lunch," Reverend Dale told them. "The women have it set up in the hall next door."

"That was very nice of them," Abigail responded. Sliding her arm through her husband's, they made their way out of the hot summer sun and toward their new married life.

It was half-past four by the time they arrived back at the ranch. Malcolm had decided to stay in town for the rest of the weekend to give them some privacy. The ladies of the church had packed them leftovers so their first night together wouldn't be spent in the kitchen.

"So, wife, what shall we do to pass the evening?" Rand asked once they'd come through the door.

She was at a loss as to how to respond. *Was he asking her to extend him his husbandly rights? Or, were they going to wait as they'd planned.*

"I suppose you could move your things back to the house. In your own bedroom, of course."

"Of course," he repeated, the two words drawing his frown.

"I mean… we did agree to take things slow. Get to know one another better. After all, it wasn't like you asked me to marry you for real."

His expression clouded over, his eyes darkened, and he gave a quick nod of his head. "I'm going to change and then head out to the barn to check on the mother and calf. Did you want to come along?"

"No, thank you. I should probably get out of this fancy dress as well, and then put away the food." She paused, then asked, "Unless you're hungry."

"We could ride out to the north pasture with a picnic lunch tomorrow, after you return from services, if you'd like."

"That sounds wonderful," she agreed. "Although, I'm pretty sure Reverend Dale is not expecting me to attend."

"I supposed not." He stalled for another few moments before saying, "Okay, then. I guess I'll get going."

Abigail was confused by his tone, by the way he clung to the doorway. *Did he want her to ask him to stay?* The memory of their shared wedding kisses came back to her in a rush. She had the sudden urge to tell him waiting wasn't necessary. She wasn't sure she was ready to be a wife in the fullest sense of the word, but she definitely wouldn't have minded another of Rand's delightful kisses.

While she was rambling on in her head, Rand left the room. She could hear him in his upstairs bedroom, shuffling across the floor, slamming draws shut and, eventually, shutting the bedroom door with a solid bang.

Too shy to ask for answers to her questions, Abigail literally ran to her bedroom and closed herself in with a gentle twist of the brass knob. She did need to get out of her beautiful violet gown and into something more appropriate for a working ranch. There'd be time later for sorting out their hastily-made plans.

If they didn't get around to talking during the picnic the next day, they had a long ride to meet with the solicitor on Monday. Surely, by then, she will have worked up the nerve to ask her husband the more intimate questions plaguing her thoughts.

Abigail awoke Sunday morning to the aroma of frying bacon and strong coffee. Rolling over in her bed—alone—she reached for her watch. Eight o'clock. She hadn't heard Rand return last evening so she must have slept more soundly than she imagined. Taking a quick minute to refresh herself, she wrapped herself in her pink satin robe and made her way to the kitchen.

"Good morning, Rand," she said. "I didn't hear you come in last night."

He turned from the stove to face her, his head lifting and falling as he took in what she was wearing. "That's because I didn't come back. I stayed in the bunkhouse."

"But I thought—"

"It was late and I didn't want to disturb you."

"While that's very considerate of you, this is your home and—now that we're legally wed—there's no reason for you to sleep anywhere but here."

The familiar twitch of his jaw drew her corresponding smile.

"Yes, ma'am," he said. "I'll be sure to move my things over after we get back from our picnic."

She inhaled deeply. "Something smells good, and different."

"It's a new tea the reverend's wife recommended," he told her. "She slipped me a packet at the wedding party."

"Really, what's it called?"

"Raspberry leaf, I think she said. It's supposed to be gentle on a woman's constitution."

"Well, it certainly does leave a pleasing aroma in the kitchen."

"I'll make you a cup if you'd like." Nodding toward the closest chair, he told her, "Take a seat. I'll make breakfast for our first morning as husband and wife."

"I could get used to this," she teased. "At least on Sundays."

"Maybe that should be our first married routine... I make you breakfast every Sunday morning."

"Me and Malcolm?"

"Oh yea, I forgot about him."

"It was very nice of him to take a room at the boarding house for the rest of the weekend, but I'm sure he'll be back bright and early tomorrow."

Rand nodded in agreement. "He'll be here in time for the two of us to check the south fence before you and I take off to see the solicitor."

"You don't need to put my name on the property deed, Rand."

"I know I don't. I just figure it'll be one more stake in your claim to Colorado as your home, and one more obstacle if they should come to try and take you away from me."

Swallowing back a lump of emotion she'd never felt before, she repeated, "From you?"

He shot her a broad smile. "Hey, housekeepers aren't easy to come by around here. When you get one you like, a man's gotta do what he can to hold onto her."

When Abigail arrived at the short corral, Rand was waiting with his handsome gelding, Bolt, and Bella, the mare he gave her as a wedding gift.

"I packed a lunch," she told him, handing him the burlap sack to affix to the pommel of his saddle. "Not much, just some cold meat and pickled vegetables, and a slice of Cyrus McCready's homemade goat cheese. And, of course, a flask of iced tea. I made it from your regular blend, rather than the raspberry leaf."

"It looks like it might rain this afternoon, so we best get going if we're gonna make it all the way up to the pasture."

The trail was most relaxing, with Bella following Bolt's lead across the even terrain. A half-hour into their ride, Rand drew to a stop beneath a copse of willow trees. "This should be good," he announced, sliding from the saddle as smoothly as melted butter over a hot biscuit.

When she would have climbed down on her own, Rand lifted his arms and cinched his hands around her waist, pulling her from the horse until she landed in front of him, toe-to-toe.

"Hello again, Missus McIver."

Abigail laid her hands flat against his broad chest. Her fingernails scored the front of his soft cotton shirt. "Hello to you too, Randall Anthony McIver."

"Are you making fun of my full Christian name?"

"Of course, not. Although, you have to admit, it is a mouthful."

"Well so is Abigail Elizabeth Willoughby McIver," he responded.

Lifting his hand to cup her cheek, his fingers slid through the loose strands of her hair. Every nerve ending in her scalp sprang to life.

"Perhaps, Rand is a better choice."

Without warning, he lowered his head and fit his mouth over hers, sealing their lips in a lengthy, and thoroughly enticing, kiss. When he leaned back and made eye contact, he told her, "And, I'll call you Abby." He smiled down at her before dusting his thumb across her lower lip. "Abby McIver. I like it."

Braver than she could ever remember being, she lifted herself up onto her tiptoes and pressed her lips to his, initiating another perfect kiss. When she came up for air, she admitted, "I like it, too."

"The name?"

"And the kisses."

Chapter Seven

Rand

While Abby carried the remnants of their half-eaten lunch into the house and changed out of her riding clothes, Rand made short work of grooming and feeding the horses.

He couldn't wait to get back inside to his bride. Those two kisses had turned to a dozen, each one sending his senses reeling and putting his desire on full alert. Despite their earlier agreement, he desperately wanted to consummate their marriage. Yet, he knew he wouldn't rush her.

Theirs was not a traditional marriage, or a love match, but rather a bargain from which they would both benefit. *Why then, if that were true, was he anxious to make her his own in every sense of the word?*

By the time he returned to the house, Abby was curled up in her favorite chair in the front parlor, her sketchbook, and pencils, in hand. The first time he'd seen one of her drawings, he'd been astounded by her talent. He liked nothing better than to sit at his desk and work, while she drew pictures of things she'd encountered throughout the day.

He'd barely taken his seat, when she turned her latest work around for his review. "What do you think?"

"It looks just like the new calf which—by the way—you still haven't named," he reminded her.

"Slick," Abby said, "for the way she just slid out of her mama's belly."

"Slick?" he repeated, not attempting to hide a full-blown laugh. "Well, I definitely wasn't expecting that."

"Good. That should keep you guessing about a lot of things."

As much as he wanted to spend the entire evening talking to Abby about any number of things, there was work to be done on the ranch's accounts. It wasn't only hard work that was needed to restore Bent River to a thriving ranch, but also money. Something he didn't have a lot of at the moment. Still, as long as he had his livestock, his home, and his new wife he was a happy man.

Perhaps, with Abigail to show him the way, he might rediscover some of the faith he'd lost among the ruins of war. She sure seemed bent on trying to bring him back to church. Considering he was willing to give her anything she wanted, he suspected finding his way back to the flock wasn't as unreasonable as he'd once assumed.

At half-past ten, Rand pushed the ledgers aside and stood to stretch. He'd moved his few personal items back to the house and put them in his room earlier. He had no excuse to return to a night of solitude in the bunkhouse.

"I'm heading to bed," he told her, drawing Abby's attention from her latest project. "I guess I'll see you in the morning."

"Rand? Wait up a minute," she called from her chair.

As always, he was undone by the silky tone of her voice. "Yes?"

"It's been a long day. A nice long day."

"Yes, I reckon it has."

She rose from her chair and came to stand in front of him, the very closeness of her making his senses come alive. When she laid her hand against his chest, he was certain she could feel the thump of his heart.

"I was thinking you can conserve some of your energy by not climbing those steep stairs to your bedroom."

He lowered his gaze and met the warmth of her huge brown eyes, and the smile on her full lips. "Are you suggesting we share a bedroom, Missus McIver?"

"Assuming you don't mind, of course."

Rand scooped her up in his arms and pressed a kiss to her lips before steering a course for the downstairs bedroom. "I'm fine with sharing, if you're sure that's what you want."

She returned his kiss with an even longer one of her own before telling him, "I don't know what I'm doing, but I do know what I want. I want you."

Abby

Oh, sweet tea!

Abby rolled over in the bed and wrapped her arms around the feather pillow where Rand had laid his head. It still smelled of him, a mixture of soap with just a hint of hay. She could hear him puttering around the kitchen, whistling a tune she couldn't quite identify.

While she'd often wondered about what the marital act might entail, in all her twenty-six years, she'd never once speculated on how it would feel. How many emotions could be released in the act of making love.

Knowing it was her first time, Rand had been

gentle, patient, and understanding. He'd coaxed her into willful submission and then unleashed a storm of both physical and emotional responses from her body.

The back door opened and closed. Muted voices could be heard. Rand and Malcolm were discussing what needed to be done while she and Rand were in Delphi speaking with the lawyer.

Forcing herself from the bed, despite her desire to sleep the day away, Abby made her way to the water closet for her morning ritual. Malcolm's arrival meant the day had begun, and she had chores to complete before they got on the road.

"Morning, Malcolm," Abby greeted when she arrived in the kitchen twenty minutes later.

"Mornin' Missus McIver," Malcolm responded, a snicker barely concealed beneath the weight of his mustache.

"It's still just Abigail," she told him, reserving 'Abby' for Rand's exclusive use.

"Rand's gone out to hitch up the buggy, but he left you some of those soft-boiled eggs you like so much. There's also tea and toast on the stove top."

"I see the two of you have managed to empty an entire pot of coffee," she said, moving the battered enamel pot to the drainboard. "This thing has seen better days," she added. "Maybe it's time to get a new one."

"Naw, don't do that. You'll get rid of all the leftover flavor," Malcolm explained. "This here pot may be old, but it's seen us through a dozen cattle drives and at least a half-dozen long winters."

"Well then, we wouldn't want to mess with perfection. Would we?"

They were on the road less than an hour later. Rand had rigged the buggy with a canopy to keep the sun from beating down on them come high noon. Abby settled in the seat and snuggled close to her husband's side.

"Why Missus McIver, are you trying to seduce me?"

"No, of course not," she responded. "At least not out here in the open."

"I admit I'm disappointed, but understand your reluctance. How about we discuss what we're going to say to the lawyer when we get there? Maybe that will keep your mind off other... more intimate... things."

"One thing's for sure, I want to ask him how I go about getting my father to ship the things I left behind. Also, I need to get access to my savings. Oh, and then there's Aunt Ginny."

"Aunt Ginny? Are we taking in a family

member?”

“No, my Aunt Ginny passed away last year. She left me a few things, and I want to have them. Especially the money.”

Rand drew the buggy to a sharp halt. “Money?” Turning to face her, he said, “I’m thinking there may be a few things we neglected to talk about in our previous conversations.”

“Don’t go getting all excited, Rand,” she told him. “I’m not even sure how much money there is since my father managed all that but, as of two days ago, it’s now *our* money.” When he looked at her with astonishment, she clarified, “I’m far more interested in getting my art supplies and at least part of my wardrobe of dresses.”

“My goodness, Abby, you are full of surprises.”

“Not really,” she admitted. “It’s just I rarely think about anything other than my art. And, now, my new husband, our home, and our life together.”

“Peter Matthews, Solicitor,” Rand read the sign affixed to the beam above the narrow doorway. “We’ve arrived.” Opening the door, he stepped back and ushered her inside.

“Mister and Missus McIver to see Mister Matthews,” he told the young man at the desk just inside the door. “I sent a telegram.”

“Yes,” the fellow acknowledged. “You’re a few

minutes early, but I'm sure he's ready for you."

Peter Matthews was not what Abby was expecting. All her father's solicitors were old men, with gray hair and long beards, and eyes as cold as a freak winter storm. Mister Matthews was young, probably not much older than Rand's thirty-three years.

"Why don't we get started with the deed to the ranch?" Matthews asked. "I understand you want to place your wife's name on the formal land claim."

"Yes," Rand confirmed. "I want her to have an equal stake in the property."

"Has Sheriff Winkle heard back from the marshal's office in Colorado Springs regarding your marriage and desire to remain in Colorado?"

"Not as of the weekend," Abby explained. "However, we would still like for you to contact my father's solicitors on our behalf. I have a few requests."

"Such as?" the solicitor asked.

Reaching into the pocket of her dress, she produced a list she'd written out just that morning. "First off, I intend to set up an account for myself and my husband at the bank in Cripple Creek. I have money in my account in Bartlesfield I want transferred over. I want you to be aware in case there are any problems with the smooth transfer."

Drawing a breath, she continued. "Next, I want my father to ship all of my art supplies, and the remainder of my clothing and personal belongings."

"Is that it?" Matthews questioned.

Abby spared a quick glance at her husband, before adding, "Finally, my recently departed aunt left me an inheritance. I'm not sure of the amount, but I know the provisions were that I was to inherit either on my thirtieth birthday, or when I married, whichever came first."

"But you don't know the total of the inheritance?"

"Not exactly. My father oversaw all the family finances. I received a monthly allowance. I also received a modest income from selling my artwork. That's what makes up the money in my savings."

"We'll need to request an accounting from both the bank and the attorney for your aunt's estate," Matthews explained. "However, since you've met the provision of marriage, there should be no problem with claiming what's due you. As for the shipment of your belongings, we can negotiate the cost for transport with your father's solicitor."

"All of my wife's requests are reasonable, though, correct?"

"As long as she's been honest about her right to these items, I see no problem in settling her demands in a most civil manner."

"Wonderful. Let's start with the property deed," Rand instructed, "and then move on from there."

Abby slid a second piece of paper across the desk. "This is the name of my bank back in Texas, and the name of my father's solicitors, both in Bartlesfield and in Fort Worth."

"That should be all I'll need to get started. I'll be in touch when there are papers to be signed, or news to report."

Rand stood, shook hands with Mister Matthews, and offered her his arm. "We'll be getting out of your way then. Abigail and I have other business back in Cripple Creek, including adding her to my bank account and opening a second one for her."

"Or," she suggested, "we could just combine everything into one."

Matthews escorted them to the door and waited on the stoop until they made their way to the wagon. Once she was seated, Rand climbed aboard and took his place at her side.

"What's going on in that beautiful head of yours, wife? I can see the wheels spinning."

"I was just thinking, what if my father puts up a fuss about my requests? He can be a stubborn man when he wants to be.

"Is that it? We'll deal with whatever comes.

Together. In the meantime, is there anything else on your mind?"

"Right now, the only thing I'm thinking about is stealing a kiss from my husband."

"No thievery required, Abby. I'll gladly give in to all your desires."

Chapter Eight

Three Weeks Later
Abigail

Abby pushed aside the window curtain over the sink and watched as a lone gray horse came up the long pathway from the road. Mister McCready's eldest son, James, sat tall in the saddle. By the time he dismounted, she was on the porch waiting.

"Good day, Missus McIver," James greeted, tipping his hat.

"Hello, James. What can I do for you today?"

"Pa sent me out with a telegram and said to tell you there's a couple of big boxes waiting for you at the store. They came by wagon earlier today." He stretched out his thin arm and handed her a wadded-up piece of paper from his vest pocket.

"Thank you. I'll be sure to send Mister McIver into town to pick up the shipment later today. It's likely your father wants to get them out of his way."

"No so much, pa, as Jacob. He stubbed his toe on one as I was getting ready to leave."

"Oh, no!" Abby twinged at the thought of the small boy's pain. "Is he okay?"

"Good enough. Pa says he deserved it for running around barefoot."

She dug into her apron pocket and produced a nickel, handing it to the boy. "Don't spend that all on candy," she warned. "Or your ma will have a fit."

"I'll get a penny bag and share it with my brothers," he told her. "Nobody wants to see mama have a fit."

Once James was back on the road, Abby unraveled the paper.

"Land good. Need to meet. PM"

The solicitor's message was disheartening. Surely her father wasn't objecting to her requests.

Rand was out in the far pasture repairing the fence. Malcolm was stuck in the barn, as both remaining cows were calving at the same time. She toyed with the idea of either going after the boxes herself, or saddling her horse and riding to Delphi on her own.

Either way, Rand would be livid when he discovered she'd taken the tasks upon herself. Not wanting to upset the near-perfect arrangement they'd come too, she laid the telegram on the countertop and returned to her first attempt at apple pie. There would be time this afternoon for she and Rand to go into town for her shipment and send a telegram to Mister Matthews to let him know when they could meet.

Rand arrived for lunch precisely at half-past twelve. Abby felt certain she could set her watch by his stomach.

"Something smells great," he said. Coming up behind her, he snaked his arms around her middle, and snuggled beneath her loose curls. "The food smells pretty danged good too." Once he'd feathered a kiss on the side of her throat, he asked. "What's for lunch?"

"I made your favorite tamale casserole," she told him. "I'm not making promises, but it does look good."

"Your skills—in every area of our home—are improving daily."

A warm flush rose in her cheeks. The man was incorrigible.

"We received a telegram from Mister Matthews," she told him. "And there are boxes at the mercantile for pick up."

"What did Matthews have to say?" Rand asked, releasing her to pour himself a cup of coffee.

"The land deed is filed but there's a problem he needs to discuss with us. I assume father's balking about releasing my inheritance. No doubt, he's leery of our marriage after I refused Mister Champion's offer."

"I'll hitch the wagon after we finish lunch and go into town for your belongings. While I'm there, I'll send a telegram saying we can be in Delphi on Thursday."

"Are you sure you can get away?"

"Like you, I want all this settled as quickly as possible. I'll make time."

"I could go with you," she suggested.

"That's okay, I can go alone. I'm sure you've got things you'd rather do here. I have to pick up a few things while I'm there for those barn repairs I mentioned yesterday."

Abby knew a moment of disappointment at Rand's claim he could go alone. A small niggle of concern worked its way up her back. Over the past week, he'd been going back out to the barn every evening, despite having worked the entire day.

Was he already tired of her? Was spending time working on some project in the barn preferable to their usual routine of evenings together in the parlor?

The thought made her senses reel. Despite the unconventional beginning to their marriage, Abby was almost certain her heart would break if Rand wanted to call an end to their relationship. After all, it hadn't taken her long to realize how deeply she cared, how easily she'd fallen in love.

Rand

Rand drew the wagon to a halt in front of the mercantile and tethered the horses to a nearby post. Not that they were likely to run with a full-size wagon and a couple hundred pounds of metalwork in the wagon's bed. Still, he wasn't taking chances, not when his cargo was so important to him.

"Afternoon Cyrus," Rand called out when he entered the store. "Abigail says you're holding some boxes for her."

"Yep," the merchant confirmed. "Came in on the early stage. Two large wooden crates, and a smaller satchel."

"If you want to point me to where they're sitting, I'll get them out of your way."

"The boys can load them up for you, Rand." Without waiting for Rand's replay, Cyrus hollered, "James, Jack, come out here."

The boys came running.

"Yea, Pa, what do you need," Jack, the younger of the two asked.

"Load those boxes and satchel on Mister

McIver's wagon out front so's your little brother will quit tripping over them."

"His toe's still smartin'," Jack offered. "However, that chunk of rock candy James gave him helped some."

"You're lucky your ma didn't see that bag your brother brought back from Myrtle's place, or she'd have taken it away. You three are going to spoil your supper," Cyrus said.

"Oh, I don't know, Cyrus," Rand added helpfully. "I don't remember a bit of sugar ever stopping me from one of Aunt Betty's suppers."

The older man chuckled. "I suppose not. Of course, you and I worked a lot harder when we were their age. Kids got it way too easy, what with only working four or five hours after their schoolin'"

"Schoolin's hard," Jack grumbled. "'specially 'rithmetic. I hate ciphers."

"A good education is important," Rand pointed out. "With it, you can do anything you want. Be anything you want."

"I want to be a soldier," James told them. "Like you were in the wars."

Rand shook his head and explained, "No, James, you don't. War is ugly. Nothing changes more than watching a man die right in front of you, for no better reason than wanting what's not his. Or, at least for not being able to share all the good Lord gave us."

Once the boys had gone off to do their father's bidding, Cyrus commented, "I think that's the most I've ever heard you say about the territorial fight."

"There's nothing wrong with being part of the military in peacetime," Rand explained. "However, it's no place to be when there's fighting."

Cyrus gave a quick nod of agreement, then asked, "How's the missus?"

"She's fine, thank you. Although, she may not be as happy with ranch life once winter sets in."

"Heck, I can't say as I'd blame her. It gets cold enough here in town. I'd not want to be out on the open range either."

"Did those supplies I ordered come in?" Rand asked. "The ones from Denver."

"About half of what you wanted. Still not sure what you're planning to paint with these narrow brushes. It'd take you a week to paint one fence post."

Rand buried a laugh. "Those are artists' brushes. They're for Abigail, just in case her father doesn't ship the ones she left behind."

"She paints?"

"I've not seen one of her paintings, but she does make pretty sketches with the pencils and charcoals she brought with her.”

“Maybe when she’s got some to sell, I could put ‘em up here in the store,” Cyrus offered. “If’n she wants to part with them.”

“I’ll be sure to ask her once the time comes.” Rand glanced around. “Can I also get eighteen inches of some of your fanciest ribbon?”

“So, the brushes are a gift, are they?”

“Yes, they are. I might as well gussy them up a bit before I give them to her.”

Their task done, James and Jack came back into the store, and made a beeline for the front counter. “Mister McIver,” Jack began excitedly. “What’s that pile of metal you got in the back of your wagon?”

“Mind your own business,” Cyrus warned.

“That’s okay, Cyrus. It’s a wood-burning kettle stove. I’ve still got to put it together, but it can be used to heat up two or three rooms at a time, instead of lighting three fireplaces. Or, lighting one and freezing in the other rooms.”

Jack shivered. “I don’t like the cold, especially when we have to walk to school.”

“Be grateful you only have to walk a half-mile,” Cyrus told them. “When I was a boy, the one-room schoolhouse was nearly two miles away. Uphill.”

“Just think though,” Rand teased. “In the winter, you could sled all the way home.”

It was nearly five when Rand arrived home. He stopped first at the backdoor and unloaded the two boxes onto the porch and then laid the leather satchel on top of them. Then, he climbed back into the wagon and dropped everything off near the bunkhouse before unhooking the wagon.

Malcolm arrived to take charge of the unbridled horses. "One more heifer and a steer. It was like those two mamas were competing for my attention, each bawling themselves senseless through the birthin'"

"Demanding, were they," Rand joked.

"So much so, Abigail came out and offered her help." Malcolm gave a sound shake of his head. "I sent her back inside. She's still not got the stomach for it, and I didn't want her upchucking all over the place."

"I'm not sure I ever want her to get the stomach for it," Rand admitted. "I'd just as soon she spent her time doing other stuff outside the stable and barn."

"Yea, like tending to some babies," Malcolm suggested. "Assuming—of course—you do what's necessary."

Rand had to admit, he'd been thinking along the same lines. Starting a family with Abby was a most agreeable idea. The thought of a couple of sons, and maybe a daughter or two, set his heart pounding. *Would they have dark brown hair like his? Or, perhaps, their mother's reddish-gold?* It didn't matter of course. He'd love them either way, same as he loved their mother.

The realization sank in like a heavy rock falling to the bottom of a still stream.

He loved Abigail Elizabeth Willoughby McIver, and probably had since she climbed out of the sheriff's wagon nearly three months earlier.

And he was fine with that.

Chapter Nine

Abigail

Abby waited patiently, or at least somewhat patiently, while Rand pulled the two crates in through the door and pried off the tops. The satchel contained her lace shawls, one of her brocade ballgowns—not that she'd have use for it here—and two pairs of high-button shoes. Also impractical for life on a working ranch.

The crates, though, were another matter entirely.

"Okay, here we go," Rand announced as the first lid came free.

Inside was one of her easels, another smaller box containing at least a dozen pots of paints, and a handful of brushes. Not as carefully packed as she would have done, the bristles were bent, and the ferrule and crimp damaged. Only the handles seemed intact.

Tears sprung to her eyes and she blinked them

back, save for this single droplet that rolled down her cheek.

The second crate held her two smaller easels and a few other random supplies. Her treasured box of oil paints was nowhere to be seen. Leave it to her father to hold back the one thing she treasured most, a birthday gift from her mother not long before she passed away.

"Is everything here?" Rand asked.

"Not quite, but the majority of what I asked for on my list."

"We'll get Mister Matthews to put in a second request," he told her. "Write up another list for what's missing."

"I will," she responded, somewhat absently as her attention had returned to her damaged brushes. She lifted one in her hand and stroked the ruined bristles with her thumb.

"I take it your brushes are ruined," he commented.

"I might be able to soak them in turpentine and reshape them, but probably not."

"Give me a second," he said, slipping back out onto the porch.

While she waited, Abby rummaged through the remaining art supplies and checked the easels for damage. When Rand returned a few minutes later, his grin was broad, and he was hiding something behind his back.

She did her best to peer around his big frame to see what he was holding.

"I was going to give you these after supper tonight, but I can't stand to see you so sad." He swooped his arm around in a grand flourish. Clutched in his grasp was a bouquet of brushes, all tied neatly with a pink flowered ribbon. "Here you go. I hope these will work."

Abby reached for his offering, turning the gift over in her hands. The tears she'd previously staunched ran freely from beneath her eyelids and down her cheeks. "How wonderful, and generous." Laying the brushes on the nearby table, she threw herself into Rand's arms. "Thank you, so very, very much. They're perfect."

"I'm glad. I was worried I'd ordered the wrong things."

She raised herself up on her toes and pressed her mouth to his, initiating a warm, emotional kiss. "These easily make up for whatever news Mister Matthews has to impart."

"Let's hope so."

Thursday brought the first rainy day they'd had in ages. Abby set out her heavier coat and bonnet.

She toyed with the idea of wearing her riding boots, rather than shoes, but finally settled on a pair of her button-top shoes.

"Are we all set?" she asked when she stepped off the porch.

"We could send word that we want to delay a day or two," Rand suggested. "It's going to be an uncomfortable ride in the rain, even with the canopy on the buggy."

"I brought my parasol as well, although if it gets windy it'll likely be more trouble than it's worth."

When she held up the yellow parasol with white lace trim, Rand gave a sound shake of his head. "There's no way I'm sticking my head under that! You can use it if you think it will help keep you dry."

"Oh, I don't know," Malcolm joked from the muddy pathway between the house and the barn. "I think you'd look mighty fetching holding onto one of those fancy contraptions."

"That's enough out of you, old man," Rand warned, a smirk lifting the corner of his mouth.

"Anything extra you need me to do while you're gone?" Malcolm asked. "Or, can I catch a nap in the bunkhouse?"

"I left sliced meat and cabbage salad in the ice box," Abby told him. "And there's a batch of oatcakes in the tin on top of the stove. Just remember to take off your boots at the door. I don't want you tracking mud on my clean kitchen floor."

"You've become quite the homemaker, Abigail," Malcolm complimented. "You're baking is top notch."

"I find it very relaxing, except when the bread won't rise."

"We'd better get going," Rand suggested. "The road's going to be slow going as it is."

Mud spattered up from behind the horses as the trudged along the soggy path. Every once in a while, Rand would have to slap the reins a bit more forcefully than usual to keep the reluctant animals moving.

"I don't blame you fellas," Abby crooned. "I'd hate to be walking through all that slimy stuff too."

"Something tells me, we're going to owe these two some extra apple slices and a really good rubdown when we get home."

"I know I plan to take a nice, hot bath," she admitted. "Assuming, of course, you're willing to wash my back."

His concentration on the road, she had to lean closer to see the smile on his face. "I'm pretty sure that can be arranged, Missus McIver, as long as you'll wash mine."

Abby's senses tingled with awareness. Perhaps

bringing up the subject of bathing wasn't the wisest thing to do out in the middle of nowhere with another three or four hours of travel yet to go.

They reached the solicitor's office within the hour, and only ten minutes late for their scheduled appointment. Not put off by their tardiness, Peter Matthews was waiting for them in the front office when they arrived.

"You two must be soaked," he commented. Turning to his assistant, he suggested, "Harold, I'm sure a pot of tea would hit the spot right now. If you wouldn't mind rustling that up."

The young man nodded, before making his way to the backroom to attend to his boss' request.

"Tea would be wonderful," Abby agreed.

"Let's go into my office and we can review what I've learned."

Rand slid his arm protectively around her back and ushered her forward. Once they were seated, Matthews slid into the chair behind his desk.

"I understand you received a shipment of two crates, and one leather satchel," he began. "And, your savings in the amount of three hundred and sixty-two dollars, and eighty cents has been transferred from Bartlesfield to Cripple Creek Savings and Loan."

"Yes, that's correct," Abby confirmed. "There

were a few things damaged during transport, and a few things missing. I've made a list."

Matthews nudged a pile of papers across the desk. "Here is your land deed, now in both names. It's been filed with the court, and the circuit judge has signed off." As soon as Rand tucked the papers into his jacket pocket, the solicitor opened a document folder on his desk. "We've run into a problem with the issue of your inheritance."

"What kind of a problem?" Abby asked.

"There isn't any money left in the account. According to the bank auditor, and your late aunt's estate attorney, most of the money has been siphoned off by your father to improve on his land holdings."

"How could that happen?" Rand asked. "Wasn't the money held in trust?"

"It was, and the auditor is looking into who at the Bartlesfield branch may have helped your father transfer money from your trust fund to his account."

Abby's stomach roiled with a mixture of anger and regret. She'd intended to use her money to help Rand build his herd. Now, there was nothing. Or next to nothing. "Was this... his stealing from me... caused by my refusal to wed Mister Champion?"

Matthews shook his head. "Not likely. As far as my counterparts in Fort Worth could tell, the two have still gone into business together and merged their ranches. His use of the money began almost immediately after the reading of your aunt's last will and testament. As a matter of fact, it was the enhancements he made to his herd that first attracted Mister Champion to the idea of business arrangement."

"So, my leaving didn't affect anything, other than ruining my father's attempt to control me, and keep me under his thumb."

"Likely," Matthews explained, "he'd worked out a deal with Champion. Once you two were married, control of your finances would fall to your new husband and he could claim he'd used your money for their joint venture. If you didn't question it, there would be no one the wiser."

Abby drew in a breath. "How much did my father take? And, more importantly, how much is left?"

"The bank is still compiling that information," Matthews explained. "They estimate he'd pilfered at least three-quarters of the initial deposit."

"What will happen to them?" Rand asked.

"Well, once the bank employee is discovered, he will be dismissed and immediately arrested. The bank will, no doubt, demand he be charged with embezzlement and fraud, especially if he was paid to provide the paperwork necessary for the withdrawals.”

“And my father?” Abby asked.

“His fate is in your hands,” Matthews told her. “If you choose to press the matter, he will face the same charges as the bank employee. However, your issue is a civil matter, and only becomes criminal once you choose to have him arrested.”

“Do you know when the auditors will be finished with their review?” Abby asked.

“I expect to hear from them by early next week.”

“I’d like to think about my next steps,” she admitted. “Obviously, I need to discuss this with my husband.”

“By all means, take all the time you need.”

“Thank you, Mister Matthews,” she told him wholeheartedly. “I appreciate everything you’ve done on my… our… behalf.”

Over the last of their tea, Abby reviewed her list of missing items, and Matthews assured her he would draft a new demand that very afternoon and get it in the late mail.

“Would you like to stop for a bite to eat before we get back on the road?” Rand asked as they were leaving the law office.

“I’m not hungry,” she said simply. “I just want to get home, take that warm bath, and curl up in our bed and think things through. I'm going to pray on it too, and hope I get the guidance I need."

"While I'm not sure if this type of legal decision is something the Almighty usually deals with, if prayer brings you peace, then we'll both pray on it. Laying charges against your own flesh and blood is a big step, and one to not be taken lightly."

"Yes, it is. Yet, he cheated me, and that's not fair either."

"You're right, Abby, it isn't. I'll back you with whatever you decide."

"Thank you. You're a good man, Rand McIver. Quite possibly the best I've ever known."

"We've come a long way from that first day, Abby. I feel in my heart of hearts, we still have a long way to go, together."

His words were music to her ears. "Well then, let's get going. Our homestead, and that warm bath, are waiting."

Rand closed his hands around her waist and lifted her into the buggy. "As you wish, wife." Pointing forward, he added playfully, "On to Bent River," before snapping the reins and setting the horses in motion.

They'd been on the road for less than twenty minutes, when Abby's stomach began to toss. Frantically, she tugged at Rand's jacket.

"Stop, please. I'm going to be sick."

Rand drew the buggy to a halt just in time for Abby to lean over the side of the buggy and toss what little was left of her breakfast onto the ground. She wiped her mouth on the sleeve of her jacket, and sat back up.

"Are you okay, darling?" Rand asked.

"Yes, I'm fine. I think my emotions have gotten the better of me. I'm sure we can go on now."

"Are you sure? I'm fine sitting here until your tummy's settled."

"Please, let's just go. I want to get home."

Rand set the buggy in motion again, this time at a much slower pace.

Abby sank back into the seat and let her mind wander. Thoughts of her childhood, her mother, her father flowed through her hand. More recent thoughts of Rand, and her life in Cripple Creek.

Whoa... wait... back up.... had her husband just called her 'darling'?"

Chapter Ten

Cripple Creek Community Church
The Following Sunday

Rand

Rand closed the distance between himself and Abby in two long strides. She was standing beneath the orange canopy of a huge oak with the reverend's wife and Sadie Winkle. They were talking about different types of tea, and what they were used for, the last part of their conversation drawing their combined laughter.

"Sorry I took so long," he apologized when he stopped at her side. "A few of the older gentlemen were regaling us with stories about my uncle and how he used to ride his mule to services, rather than his horse, and then complain about being late."

"We've all heard the stories," Adelaide Dale told them. "Many, many times."

"Your uncle sounds like a good man," Abby said. "I'm sorry I didn't get to meet him."

"He'd have loved you," Rand predicted. "Maybe even more than he loved his church."

"I'd venture his love of his church," Sadie said, "far outweighed his interest in his ranch. Or nearly anything else for that matter."

"You'd be right about that," he confirmed. "It's been a couple years now, and I'm still digging my way out, and rebuilding things from the ground up."

He caught a glimpse of Abby as he spoke, her complexion going pale, her lower lip held between her teeth as she worried the flesh with tiny nibbles. Something was bothering her, yet he couldn't pinpoint what it was.

"Are you ready to go home?" he asked. "Or, did you want to visit some more?"

"I'm ready," she confirmed. "I've got a roast in the oven, and need to add vegetables to the pot."

They were halfway between the church and home, when he asked, "Is something troubling you, Abby?"

"No, of course not. Why would you ask that?"

"You seemed a bit upset when I mentioned all the work that I'm doing to rebuild Bent River."

"It's just... well... you've stopped spending evenings with me in the parlor, choosing instead to work out in the barn. I'm worried you've tired of our marriage." She drew a breath, and added, "Not that I expect you to spend all your free time with me. I mean… after all… we had an arrangement."

Rand pulled the buggy off on the side of the road and turned to face his wife. When he reached for her, she slipped easily into his embrace. "Don't ever mistake my putting in a few extra hours each day as indifference to our union. Even though we started out as an agreement to keep you from having to go back to Texas, I think we both realize there's more to this than just business, or convenience. Or, at least I have."

Abby snuggled more deeply into his arms and laid her head on his shoulder, and her hand against his chest. Even through the thickness of his heavy plaid shirt, he could feel the warmth of her touch. The beat of his heart picked up speed.

"I have felt the same. I'd hoped to show my appreciation by sharing my inheritance so you could enlarge the herd sooner than planned. Or, you could use it to hire another man to help with the work. However, now, I fear there's little I bring to this marriage."

He raised her chin on the very tips of his fingers until their gazes met. When he bent forward and pressed a gentle kiss to her lips, a single tear rolled down her cheek. "Abigail," he began, needing to emphasize what he was going to say. "You bring more than you'll ever know to our lives, our home. You bring light, happiness, warmth. If I've given you the wrong idea about how I feel having you around, I'm sorry."

"Let's go home, Rand." Cupping his jaw in her hand, she drew him back for another kiss. "There are a few places where I know we connect perfectly. Perhaps we should spend the afternoon exploring them."

Later that day, Rand made his way to the barn to complete the very minimal, although necessary, tasks. His body still thrummed with the memory of their afternoon lovemaking. It was a good thing Malcolm had stayed in town for the evening, as Rand felt certain his good friend would know exactly what he and Abby had been up to.

The project he'd been working on for the past month was nearly complete, and his extra hours away from Abby would soon come to an end. Hopefully, she'd be as pleased with what he'd created as she would be with the return of their extra together time.

Now, if only they could get things with her father settled. They hadn't broached the subject of what she was going to do, and he couldn't help but wonder. As soon as they heard from Peter Matthews, a decision would have to be made, albeit a difficult one no matter which route Abby chose to take.

Abigail

Abby was outside hanging bed sheets on the clothesline when James McCready pulled up on his horse. She set the basket aside, and met him at the gate.

"Hello, James, what have you got for me today?"

He passed her another crumpled piece of paper. "Telegram, ma'am."

She took the paper from his grasp. "Give me a second to grab you a couple of pennies."

"No need, Missus McIver," James said. "Our ma took away our candy bag and is doling it out slow and easy. I got no need for more money, at least not today."

Abby chuckled. "I'll keep that in mind for the next time you have to ride out here for a delivery."

The boy doffed his battered hat and reined his horse around to leave. "Pa said to tell you that the things you ordered from Denver should be here on Friday."

"Let him know I'll be in to get them that afternoon, or the next day."

Once James rode away, Abby unfolded the message and read it aloud. "*News. Will stop in Tue morn. Peter.*"

The solicitor's impending visit meant she'd have to make a decision on what to do about her father's duplicity. As angry as she was, Abby wasn't sure she could send her own father to jail.

Over supper that evening, Abby asked, "Rand, what do you think I should do about my father?"

"It's not my decision but, if it helps you work things out, know that your inheritance—if there is any left—has nothing to do with us. Extra money would have been nice, but I'm confident I can turn this ranch around with or without it, especially with you by my side. You do what your heart tells you to do." He hesitated, then added, "As long as it doesn't mean going back to Texas."

"I've no intention of leaving Cripple Creek, or you."

"Good. Let's wait and see what Mister Matthews has to report, and then you can make your decision."

It was nearly ten when Peter Matthews' buggy pulled into the yard. Rand had hovered nearby all morning so he could be there to support her during her decision. While he greeted the solicitor, Abby made a pot of tea and set out some scones she'd bought at Miss Myrtle's Café the day before.

"Take a seat," Rand said, motioning Matthews toward the kitchen table. "If you'd prefer, we can go to the parlor, but I thought you might need some room if you have papers to share."

"This is fine," Matthews told them. "Since I'm expected in Colorado Springs this afternoon, I'm eager to get down to business."

"What have you learned?" Abby asked.

"I received a written report from my associate in Fort Worth. The bank auditor has finished his exam. The initial inheritance was twelve-hundred dollars, of which your father has spent eight-hundred and forty, leaving the account a balance of three-hundred-twenty dollars. Since you've met the criteria for the release of the funds with your marriage, the remaining money will be forwarded to your account here in Cripple Creek."

"Honestly," Abby admitted, "that's more than I was expecting to have left." She shot Rand a quick smile, grateful there was at least something she could contribute to Bent River. "Is there more?"

"We've unearthed a few other details regarding your father's agreement with Mister Champion, but they're not really related to your claims, so it's up to you if you want to hear them or not."

"Other than to explain why my father wanted to

trade me for a deal, and why a man I barely knew wanted to make me his bride, I've no interest at all."

"Let's just say, Mister Champion had no interest in a traditional marriage. He's since found himself a wife who will give him the respectability he needs, yet not demand anything from him he's not willing to give."

She let the solicitor's words sink in. "Well then, it seems I saved myself even more heartache by running away."

"All that's left is for you to decide whether or not you want to press charges against your father for embezzling your money."

Abby closed her eyes and let the import of what she was about to say wash over her, through her. Rand took her hand in his and gently squeezed before running his thumb across the backs of her fingers, showing her—without words—his unflinching support. Every scripture verse regarding honesty and forgiveness that she'd ever read came back to her in a flash.

When she opened her eyes, she met the solicitor's serious gaze. "I will not be pressing charges against my father. However, I do have a couple of final conditions."

A minute smile lifted the corners of her husband's lips, and Abby relaxed in the knowledge her decision had pleased him.

"I'll be more than happy to convey your decision, as well as your stipulations."

"First of all, I want him to ship the remainder of my personal possessions, especially the box of watercolors my mother gave me on my last birthday. And, I want them packed with diligence so that nothing is damaged." Sparing another smile for Rand, she added, "And second, in recompense for the money he stole from me, I want Horace."

"Horace?" both the attorney and Rand repeated at the same time.

"My father's prize-winning bull. He's to be shipped immediately so he arrives before winter sets in." Turning to Rand, she explained, "I know you intended to purchase a bull for the herd in the spring. This will be one expense we won't have to worry about."

"So, let me get this straight," Mister Matthew clarified. "You want the rest of your personal belongings, such as clothes, jewelry, and items given to you as gifts. You want a set of watercolor paints given to you by your late mother. And, you want your father's bull, named Horace. In exchange for these items, you'll release your father from any indemnity and agree to not press charges for theft."

"Yes, that's correct."

"Excellent," Matthews responded. "I'll send a formal letter off to my counterpart in Fort Worth after my meeting in Colorado Springs."

Once he'd finished making notes of their conversation, Peter Matthews finished his tea and scone and excused himself. Rand walked him to his buggy while Abby stood watch from the doorway.

"Whew!" she exclaimed when Rand returned to her side. "I'm happy to have this mess out of the way."

He wrapped his arm around her shoulders and pulled her close. Pressing a kiss to the top of her head, he told her, "You did good, Abby. While what your father did was wrong, forgiving him will give you the peace you deserve, even if it doesn't ease his conscience."

"I am at peace. I just hope my father sees this as a gift and doesn't balk at my requests."

"I don't see why he wouldn't. Jail time would have ruined him completely. He'd likely forfeit his home. If you ask me, he's getting off easy."

"I'm hoping, in time, my father and I can have a relationship of some sort. I don't expect it'll ever be easy, but it would be nice to be able to communicate from time-to-time."

"This has been a big day," he pointed out. "I say we celebrate by going to the harvest square dance at the church hall a week from Saturday. You can show off one of your fancy ball gowns."

"Will you wear your Sunday suit and tie?" Wagging her eyebrows, she told him, "You look very handsome when you're all decked out."

Somewhat self-consciously, she suspected, he reached up and touched the scar on his upper lip. "Handsome, you say? I don't think I've ever been called handsome before."

Abby slid her fingertip over the scar. "Then, you've obviously been talking to the wrong women."

Chapter Eleven

Cripple Creek Community Hall
Harvest Festival Dance
Ten Days Later

Rand

Rand tugged at the tie around his neck and wished he'd not been so eager to please his wife. Now that Abby had convinced him he'd find an inner contentment if he returned to the church, he'd been going with her every Sunday. Having to wear a suit to services once a week should be plenty of dressing up.

Yet, when he looked across the width of the room at his beautiful wife, dressed in a pale blue gown, her hair piled in soft curls atop her head, he realized he'd willingly do whatever—wear whatever—she asked in an effort to please her.

"You're a lucky man, Rand," Cyrus McCready said when he took his place along the wall with the other men. "She's an attractive woman, and talented too. That first painting she placed at the mercantile sold within an hour."

"Really?"

"Yep, Wanda Brewster snapped it up as soon as she laid eyes on it. Claimed she needed to add some class to her place since most her do-dads are things Cal made at the livery out of metal scrap."

Cyrus' comment drew Rand's laugh. "He once made me an ashtray for those infernal cigars Malcolm smokes. Told me it would be safe to use in the barn. Since it was heavy and deep, it wouldn't turn over and start a fire."

"Do you use it?" Cyrus asked.

"Not in the barn," Rand confirmed. "No way I'm going to risk my livestock."

"The music's about to start up again," Cyrus noted. "You gonna spin the wife of yours around the floor?"

"I'm not sure she'll appreciate me stepping on her toes, but I promised I'd give it a good try."

When the musicians returned to the stage, Rand pushed himself away from the wall and made his way across the crowded room, his gaze set on Abby. He might not be the world's best dancer but, the thought of holding his wife in his arms, gave him courage.

"Abigail," he said softly when he came up

behind her. "I believe I owe you a dance."

She turned and stepped into his arms. "That you do, Mister McIver. That you do."

Abigail

It was nearly eleven-thirty before things began winding down. Abby wished she'd worn a more comfortable pair of shoes. While she loved her fashionable satin slippers, they didn't offer a lot of support when one was being twirled around the floor to raucous fiddle music. Her tooled leather boots and one of her gingham dresses would have been far more appropriate for the evening's festivities.

There was a midnight lunch planned and she'd contributed her new favorite recipe, sweet potato squares. Once the music stopped, the men began moving tables and chairs into place. Abby joined the other women in the kitchen to help set out the trays of food.

"Abigail, how are you enjoying that raspberry tea?" Adelaide Dale asked.

Abby turned to respond when she noticed at least three other women standing there waiting for her answer, Sadie Winkle among them. "It's delicious. I took your suggestion and have it nearly every evening before bed. It definitely relaxes me."

"That's all it does?" Beatrice Williams wondered.

"Yes," Abby responded. "What else was it supposed to do?"

"That's it, dear," Adelaide assured her.

Once Adelaide and Beatrice left the kitchen with food for the buffet, Abby turned to Sadie. "What was that all about?"

"Don't mind those two," Sadie told her. "They've got it in their heads that raspberry tea is helpful to get a woman in the family way."

"Sounds like an old wife's tale to me. And, while I'm fairly new to this, I don't think tea, raspberry or otherwise, has a thing to do with it."

"Tell me about it," Sadie responded. "I never drank any raspberry tea, and I got three younguns at home, all under the age of six."

Abby poked Sadie in the side with a gentle elbow, and then leaned in close. "Sounds as if the sheriff's a straight shooter."

Sadie's laughter echoed throughout the cramped hall.

"What were you and Sadie talking about?" Rand asked when they settled in at one of the tables with their plates of food. "I don't think I've ever seen Sadie so amused."

"We were comparing notes on raspberry tea and making babies."

The look on Rand's face was comical. "Are you? I mean… are you expecting?"

Abby met his gaze, and asked, "Would you be happy if I were?"

"It's not something we've talked about, but I'd be lying if I said I hadn't given it some thought," he admitted.

"Me too… thought about it that is."

"So? You're not?"

"No, I'm not, at least not that I know of." She took his hand in hers and lifted it to her lips. "I'd thought I might be that time I got sick on our drive back from Delphi, but it turned out to be only my nerves getting the better of me."

"I'd be right pleased having a son, or two. Maybe a daughter," he told her. "Of course, you've got some say in it, too."

"I've always assumed I'd have children someday. I'm not getting any younger, after all."

He chuckled. "Neither am I. Maybe we should take our advancing years into consideration and get busy."

"When would you like to begin?" she asked,

offering him her most innocent smile.

Rand pushed his plate aside and then did the same with hers. "Turns out, I'm not hungry after all. We should probably head home."

"Mister McIvor, you read my mind."

Abby woke up the following Monday morning and took a long, leisurely stretch before rolling over in the bed and reaching for Rand's empty pillow. He'd certainly made good on his promise of getting down to business with their baby making. In an effort to help their endeavors, she intended to drag out her calendar and check the date of her last monthly.

She remembered an article she'd once read on the best times in the month to conceive. She wasn't sure if there was any sense to what the author wrote, but it couldn't hurt to follow his suggestions... just in case. With her twenty-seventh birthday coming up in two days, she figured she needed any advantage she could get.

She was in the middle of baking a batch of bread later that morning when a rumbling sound came from somewhere out in the yard. By the time she reached the porch, a huge, enclosed wagon was being backed into place by the short corral.

When the driver jumped down to the ground,

Rand was there to meet him, Abby not far behind. It wasn't until she reached where the man stood that she realized who he was.

"Tucker, it's good to see you." Motioning toward Rand, she introduced the two men. "Rand, this is Tucker Gibbons, my father's foreman. Tucker, this is my husband, Rand McIver."

The two shook hands. "Nice to meet you, McIver," Gibbons said. His attention back on her, he said, "Your father said to tell you he misses you and congratulations on your marriage."

Although she was skeptical, she responded. "Tell him *thank you* for me, please."

"Where do you want me to put this cranky bastard?" Tucker asked. "He's been shoving his weight around all the way from Bartlesfield."

"I take it this is Horace," Rand guessed.

"All sixteen-hundred-eighty pounds of him," Tucker confirmed. "And he's as ornery as all git out. Apparently, he's not a fan of riding hundreds of miles in a big box."

"Let's get him unloaded into one of the back stalls in the barn," Rand suggested. "We can reinforce it with some spare beams for the night and then Malcolm and I will look at building him a larger pen. Once he's calmed down, we'll put him out with the rest of the herd. The sooner he gets used to the other cattle, the better."

"I'll make some lunch while you fellows are tending to Horace," Abby suggested.

"You're cooking?" Tucker asked, a smirk lifting his handlebar mustache.

"I'll have you know, Tucker Gibbons, I'm a very good cook. Well... I'm a passable cook. I've not poisoned anyone yet."

"I can't wait to tell Maggie. She swore the only thing you'd ever learn how to make is your pa's chili."

Tucker left to get back on the road shortly after they finished lunch. Before he left, he retrieved a small crate from beneath the bench in the front of the wagon. Inside was the set of watercolors, another dozen or so pots of paint, and at least a dozen sketchbooks, all half-filled with drawings.

"What's this?" Rand asked, as he thumbed through the pages of the largest book.

"That's Trickle Falls, on the back side of our property where he comes up on the river. My mother and I used to pack a lunch basket and sit there for hours. She'd be doing her needlework, I'd draw."

"Nice. I'm guessing there are a few things you'll miss about your home."

"I used to love it but, once my mother died, it

was just another place. My father and I never really had much to do with one another. I sometimes think he always regretted not having a son and being stuck with a daughter who had very little interest in his big dream of being the biggest cattle rancher in all of Texas."

"And how do you feel about cattle ranching now?" Rand asked.

"I've become much more involved. Of course, that's likely because I get along so well with the ranch's owner."

"Well, yes, I suppose there's that."

Chapter Twelve

Rand's Birthday Surprise
Two Days Later

Abigail

Abby awoke to the sound of the bedroom door opening. When she looked up through sleep-glazed eyes, Rand stood there with a tray balanced on his arm.

"Good morning, Abby. I've brought you breakfast in bed."

"What?" she mumbled, wiping her eyes.

"Happy birthday, my beautiful wife."

She pushed herself into a seated position and leaned against the pillows. "Thank you, Rand. I can't believe you brought me breakfast."

"Today's all about you," he told her. "Malcolm's going to take care of everything around here, and I've got our entire day planned."

"You have? What are we doing?"

He shook his head, and told her, "It's a

surprise."

When he set the tray in her lap, Abby pulled in a long breath. He smelled wonderful, enticing. The thought of tossing the tray of food aside and pulling him down onto the bed sent a warm flush of embarrassment to her cheeks.

"You smell nice," she told him.

"Must be those fancy bath salts I found among that box of things Mister Gibbons dropped off the other day."

"I'm pretty sure none of my bath salts give off an aroma of pine trees and musk."

"Oh, that," he teased. "That's some shaving cream I haven't used in ages."

"I like it," she told him. "Very much."

"Don't go getting any ideas about seducing me," he warned. "We've got things to do that don't include making love. At least not yet, anyway."

"I'm a patient woman," she told him. "To a point."

"While you're enjoying your soft-boiled eggs, toasted bread with jam, and tea, I'm going to run you a fresh tub of water. With the proper salts of course."

"What should I wear for our day?"

"One of your flowery dresses will do just fine."

Once her bath was ready, Abby literally flew

from the bed in her excitement to get her day started. She'd not had a birthday celebration since the last one two years earlier with her mother and, the realization that Rand intended to devote the entire day to her, made this one extra special.

When she reached the kitchen an hour later, Malcolm was waiting for her, a bouquet of flowers clutched in his weathered grasp.

"Happy birthday, little bit," he told her, extending his hand to pass her his gift. "Rand's bringing the buggy around. He said to tell you he's ready to go whenever you are."

"Where's he taking me?"

"Uh, uh. There's no way I'm spillin' the beans."

"Thank you for watching over things," she told him sincerely. "It means a lot to me knowing Rand won't be worried about the ranch, and can enjoy the day too."

"My pleasure, Abigail. Now you go on and git outta here and don't keep Rand waiting. I'll stick these flowers in water for you."

Abby settled into the front seat of the buggy and laid a lightweight blanket over her lap. Tugging on the lapels of her cape, she wrapped it snuggly around her shoulders before tying her bonnet in place. Fall was now here with a vengeance, the trees barren of their colorful leaves. The mornings were frosty more often than not.

"Are you ready?" Rand asked.

"I suppose so, given you won't tell me where we're going, or what we're doing."

"Trust me. We're going to have a good time."

Rand pulled out on the road and turned toward town. Abby's heart soared. Today might be the perfect time to tell her husband exactly how she felt, how she couldn't imagine ever existing without him in her life.

The road leading through Cripple Creek was fading behind them when she finally asked, "We're not stopping in town?"

Rand gave a simple shake of his head, but didn't say anything. Rather, he gave the reins another snap and the two large horses picked up their speed.

"I packed a flask of hot tea if you need to warm up a bit," he told her finally. "There's also some apples and a bag of Missus McCready's nut and berry mix you like so much."

"I'm fine, but I'll pour you some tea if you'd like."

"No tea, but there is a second flask of coffee if you don't mind fixing me up a cup."

"Of course. Are you warm enough or would you like to share the blanket?"

"I'm fine. This sheepskin jacket is as warm as

Cyrus claimed. I'm glad he talked me into buying it."

"This must be an occasion," she teased. "Not only are you wearing your new jacket, but your best Stetson, and you even shined your boots."

"Only the best for my wife," he told her.

Shortly after noon, they pulled up to the Grandview Hotel in Colorado Springs. Once he'd secured the horses, Rand helped her down onto the wooden sidewalk. "I thought we'd have lunch here at the hotel, then do a little shopping."

"That sounds perfect," she told him, looping her arm through his. "I'm starving."

He chuckled. "You do seem to have developed a healthier appetite lately."

"What can I say? I'm starting to enjoy my own abilities in the kitchen."

After lunch, they strolled along the main street of town, stopping every once in a while to check out the myriad of different shops the larger town had to offer. "A butcher shop?" Abby said, staring at the cuts of meat hanging in the window. "Imagine that, not having to do all the work yourself."

"I'm fine with raising and then butchering my own meat, thank you. Seems like a waste of good money to pay for something you can do yourself."

They strolled a bit farther down the road when Rand stopped suddenly. When Abby looked up, her jaw dropped in surprise.

"They have an art gallery," she said, her voice filled with excitement. "Right here in Colorado Springs."

"Yes, I guess they do," Rand responded, his jaw twitching with his words.

"Can we go inside?"

"Of course. It's one of the reasons I brought you here."

When they stepped through the door, a bell chimed and a tall man in a dapper suit rushed to greet them. "You must be Mister and Missus McIver," the man said. "We've been waiting for you."

Abby's gaze shifted from the stranger to her husband and back again. "You were expecting us?"

"Mister Colin Pearson," Rand acknowledged. "It's nice to finally meet you, too. This is my wife, Abigail."

Colin Pearson reached out and grasped Abby's hand in his. "It's a pleasure, Abigail McIver."

A flutter filled Abby's stomach. *What was going on? How did Rand know this man?*

"Come on," Pearson coaxed. "Let me show you around. I think you'll really like what we did with our display."

"What display?" Abby asked.

"You're paintings, of course."

Swallowing back on her emotions, she repeated, "My paintings?"

At her side, Rand was fighting back his grin.

"I realize we only have three at the moment but, I'm hoping you'll allow us to display more when the time comes."

Rand leaned close to her side, and whispered, "Please don't be upset with me."

"I honestly don't know what to say," she stammered. When Pearson came to a stop along the back wall, Abby saw three of her landscapes hanging there. "How?"

"It took a bit of secrecy," Rand admitted. "Between me, Malcolm, and Bill, we got it done. After you repacked them in their crate because there was no room to display them at home, I snuck them out of the house. Malcolm took them into Cripple Creek, and then Bill and Sadie brought them here on Monday afternoon."

"The moment I saw them," Mister Pearson said, "I knew I had to make room in my gallery."

"Mister Pearson and I communicated by telegram at first and then I sent him one of your sketchbooks. After that, he insisted on displaying your work."

"I wasn't sure if you wanted to sell them or not,

so at the moment, they're on display," the gallery owner told her. "If you'd like to set a price, my commission is ten percent. The buyer pays the cost of shipping if necessary."

"Can I think about it for a while? I sold a few things back in Texas, mostly to neighbors, but never imagined my work would be in a gallery."

"Why not, my dear?" Pearson asked. "You've got a wonderful eye for nature." He motioned around the adjacent area. "I can make room for two more of the same size, if you have them available."

"This is all so exciting, yet a bit frightening," Abby whispered. Turning to Rand, she raised her gaze to his. "Thank you for this perfect birthday surprise. It means so much to me that you believe in my work."

"How could I not? As Mister Pearson said, you have an eye for nature. And, as far as I can see, an extraordinary talent."

Dusk was settling in by the time they got back to the ranch. Abby stirred at Rand's side, where she'd fallen asleep with her head resting on his broad shoulder.

"Are we home?"

"Yes, we are sleepyhead," he confirmed.

"I'm going to make us a sandwich and warm up

a pot of soup for supper. After that, I think you're due a proper thank you for my birthday surprise."

Chuckling, he told her, "We're not quite done yet, darling."

Darling. The endearment sank deeply into her soul.

"There's more?"

"One last present."

She couldn't imagine what else there could be, especially when Rand kept going past the house and stopped the buggy between the old cabin that was once going to be her home, and the barn.

"Where are we going?" she asked.

"Patience," he teased. He lifted her down from the buggy and grasped her hand in his, leading toward the cabin.

Smoke billowed from a chimney she'd never noticed before. On closer inspection, she realized the narrow porch and front door had been covered with a fresh coat of whitewash.

"Rand? What's all this?"

He drew her up the stairs, and opened the door, coaxing her across the threshold. "Your new studio, Abby, with windows that let in the sunlight and face the pasture. Far more room than you had in the parlor, and even a wood-burning stove so you can work out here in the winter."

She turned full circle, arms akimbo, in the middle of the largest room. Tears sprung from her eyes and rolled freely down her cheeks. The moment their gazes met again, she realized he was fighting back tears of his own. Abby launched herself into his embrace, and he pulled her tight against his chest.

"You are the most wonderful man in the world, Rand McIver. I love you with all my heart."

"You love me?"

"To quote my husband's earlier words, 'how could I not'? You're generous, gentle, and the kindest man I've ever known."

His breath came out in a rush. The tears he'd been battling welled up, and a single drop ran down his cheek. "I love you too, Abigail Elizabeth. More than you'll ever know."

She made another quick perusal of the beautiful cabin, and then suggested, "How about we douse this fire and head back to the house? Like I said, I owe you the biggest thank you of all time." She paused for a brief moment, then added, "As soon as we've had our sandwiches and soup. I'm as hungry as a spring bear."

Epilogue

Abby's Not So Surprise, Surprise
Three Years Later

Rand

Abby hung her head over the bathroom sink, obviously waiting for another wave of nausea to pass. Rand, feeling absolutely helpless, stood at the door.

"Abby, darling, are you sure you're okay?"

"Why wouldn't I be fine? It's not like this is my first time with my head hanging over the bowl."

As if on cue, their two and half year-old son, Max, bound into the bedroom. "Sissy crying," he announced.

Rand pushed away from the door jam. "I'll go get her." Staring down at his son, he ordered, "You stay here by mama until I get back."

"Mama sick?"

"Something like that," Abby grumbled. "But just as it did twice before, it'll go away. Eventually."

Rand returned moments later, their thirteen-month-old daughter, Rebecca balanced on his hip. "There you go, sweetie," he cooed to the little girl who was the spitting image of her mother. "No need to fuss."

Abby raised her head and shot him a look he knew better than to question. She needed privacy, and didn't want to alarm the children with her queasy stomach.

"Why don't I take you two downstairs for some lunch now that sissy's up from her nap?"

Max grabbed onto his free hand and tugged. "I want cookies."

"How about a sandwich and some of mama's homemade applesauce?"

Rand was in the middle of wiping the children's sticky hands and faces when Abby finally appeared in the doorway. "Did they eat everything?" she asked.

"Max ate his sandwich and most of his applesauce. Becca had noodles and applesauce." Nodding toward the closest chair, he asked, "What can I get for you?"

"Short of figuring out how I can sleep through the next six months, nothing other than a cup of herbal tea." Staring directly into his eyes, she told him, "*Not* the raspberry leaf. If anything, throw that stuff out."

He shot her a broad grin. "It's not the tea, Abby, darling."

"It's not? Are you sure?" Her teasing, coy smile undid his senses and reminded him of exactly what was to blame for his wife's current condition.

"Positive. I got rid of it myself right after Rebecca was born."

The End

Chapter One

Winter Cotillion
Hildebrand House
Boston Area Known as Back Bay
February 12, 1892

Lily Marie O'Halloran turned full-circle in the ornate ballroom of the newly built home belonging to Arthur Hildebrand, one of Boston's most prominent businessmen. As lovely as her own Beacon Hill home was, Hildebrand House was exquisite.

The marble floors glistened. Despite being trod upon by a huge number of Boston elite who had turned out for the winter cotillion. Chandeliers fitted with Mister Edison's electric candles glowed brightly above the crowd.

"Isn't it absolutely beautiful?" Cassie, Lily's younger sister, commented.

"Yes," Lily confirmed. "Lovely indeed." She scanned the room one last time before adding, "Mister Hildebrand has definitely outdone everyone with this fancy new home."

"Do you suppose William will be here?" Cassie asked. "I know he's away at university, but I thought—"

"According to mother, the entire Hildebrand family will be in attendance." Beneath her breath, Lily muttered, "Unfortunately."

Cassie swatted playfully at Lily's arm. "Don't be like that. I know you tire of mother's matchmaking efforts, but would it be so horrible to marry into such an affluent family?"

"I'm happy to leave that honor to you and Becca. After all, there are only two sons, so it stands to reason the two of you, at eighteen and twenty, would be far more suitable matches."

"But you should marry first," Cassie insisted.

Lily let loose a most unladylike snort of laughter. "It's sweet of you to think so, Cassie. But, at twenty-six, I'm a bit too far on the shelf. Any man of means or breeding isn't going to want to stake his future on me."

"But Rupert is at least six years older than you. Surely, he wouldn't be put off by your age. You're beautiful, talented—you play the piano far better than Becca and me—and you're smart."

"And, as our mother so often likes to point out, I'm also opinionated, outspoken, and a pain in the bustle. Not that I would wear one of those foul contraptions."

"Speaking of mother," Cassie whispered, "here she comes, with Mister Hildebrand and Rupert in tow."

The three of them came to a stop in front of Lily and Cassie. Rupert bowed at the waist, and lifted both Cassie's and Lily's fingers to his lips for a brief kiss. "Good evening, ladies. Are you enjoying yourselves so far?"

"Everything is lovely," Cassie gushed.

"Very nice," Lily agreed. "I do believe the majority of Boston proper are in attendance."

"Exactly as I'd planned," Arthur Hildebrand bragged, his gaze raking her from head-to-toe as he spoke. "There's no sense owning such a fine home if you're not going to show it off."

Wanting to escape the strange way Mister Hildebrand was leering at her, Lily turned to her mother and asked, "Where's papa and Becca? I haven't seen them since we arrived."

Eleanor O'Halloran swept her arm wide, encompassing the whole of the massive ballroom.

"Your father is doing his duty by chaperoning your sister while she's out on the ballroom floor with Mister William Hildebrand.

At Lily's side, Cassie gave a soft whimper. Cassie had been head-over-heels for the youngest Hildebrand son since they first met summer before last at the Hildebrand's lakeside vacation home. Obviously, her mother's matchmaking efforts had paired up the wrong daughter with the soon-to-be solicitor.

Rupert settled his dark gaze on Cassie, totally oblivious to her distress. "Miss Cassandra, I was hoping I could escort you to the dancefloor as well."

Cassie recovered quickly. Blinking back any show of upset, she flashed Rupert a demure smile. "I'd be delighted."

Lily's breath came out on a sigh of relief. While she felt bad for her sister, the realization that the eldest Hildebrand son had set his cap for Cassie rather than her, made Lily immensely happy. Rupert was all right, she supposed, but she felt nothing other than a passing friendship toward the man.

He was definitely handsome. Successful. Poised to take over the family business some day, he was most assuredly a fine catch. Assuming a woman was interested only in the trappings of an arranged marriage. Lily, had no such interest. She preferred to remain single her entire life rather than marry for money, position, or to avoid being labeled a spinster.

"They make a striking couple, don't they?" Her mother's question was aimed directly at Arthur Hildebrand.

The widower nodded his agreement, then focused his attention back on Lily. "What do you think, Miss O'Halloran? Is a match between Rupert and Miss Cassandra, and my younger son William and Miss Rebecca, not an excellent arrangement for both our families?"

"I suppose," Lily agreed grudgingly. "Despite the fact that arranged marriages went out with the Victorian bathwater."

"Lily Marie!" Eleanor scolded.

Much to Lily's and her mother's surprise, the senior Hildebrand broke into laughter. "I'd heard you were outspoken, Miss Lily, but I believe this is the first time I've been witness to your refreshing honesty."

"And I'm most appreciative of the fact you weren't offended, sir," Lily told him. "I get so tired of apologizing."

"At fifty-five, I'm far too old... too experienced... to be easily offended." Turning toward her mother, he added, "I believe our previous discussion—your suggestion—is perfectly acceptable and exactly what I need."

A knot twisted inside her gut, but Lily dared to ask, "What suggestion?"

Her mother lifted Lily's hands in hers and squeezed tightly. "A match of course. Between you, our eldest daughter, and Mister Arthur Hildebrand."

Lily's gaze shot from her mother to the widower and back again. "Have you lost your mind, mother?" Biting her lip, she offered, "Again, no offense intended, Mister Hildebrand, but I've no intention of marrying a man old enough to be my father."

His steely gray stare narrowed in her direction. "I guarantee you, young lady, I'm still in the prime of my life for the more important aspects in a marital relationship."

Lily swallowed the lump forming in her throat and gave a sound shake of her head. "I truly don't know what to say. Other than *absolutely not*." Swiveling around, she made a dash for the closest door. Over her shoulder, she called out, "I'll hire a ride home, mother. Stay and enjoy your triumph in matching your two youngest daughters."

Thirty minutes later, Lily was rushing through the door of her Beacon Hill home and up the stairs to her corner bedroom. Emmaline, her lady's maid, followed closely behind.

"Miss Lily, what's the matter? Why are you home so early, and by yourself?"

"I had to get out of there," she insisted. "My mother was about to marry me off, and I couldn't stand being there for another moment."

The young maid pursed her lips in an obvious

effort to hold in her laughter. Lily was not as easily amused. Having been her maid for nearly a decade, Emmaline had been a witness to all of Lily's previous matchmaking disasters.

"I know your mother can be pushy, Miss Lily, but she has your best interests at heart. She wants to see you married and settled into your own home. To have your own family." Almost as an afterthought, she asked, "Who was it this time? Rupert Hildebrand? Or, were her sights set on another of the Boston upper crust?"

"Oh, much, much worse," Lily said, not waiting for Emmaline's help in shrugging out of her fancy ballgown. "She all but promised me to Arthur Hildebrand."

"Old man Hildebrand," Emmaline gasped. "He's old enough to be your father."

"Exactly what I told them. Just before I fled the party."

"While I can certainly understand your reluctance in this instance, you know she's not going to stop until she's found you a husband."

"I've got to get out of here. Not just this house, but all of Boston. I've got money, thanks to my inheritance from Nana Watson. Perhaps, I'll go to Chicago."

"And what would you do once you're there?" Emmaline asked. "It's not as if you've got any special training, other than time spent at that snobby finishing school, and being a high society debutante."

Lily rolled her eyes and shrugged her shoulders, letting the honesty of her maid's assessment sink in. "I'm smart, as my darling sister pointed out earlier tonight. I can learn anything I need to in order to get by. You could come with me. At my expense, of course."

Emmaline shook her head. "No, thank you. I appreciate the offer, but I've met someone and we've become close. He's a foreman at the textile factory, a hardworking and good man. I'm hoping he'll ask for my hand."

"How wonderful," Lily told her honestly. "I wish you the best, of course."

"If you're serious about escaping your family home, what about something a little farther west?"

"How much farther?" Lily asked, a bit apprehensive yet curious.

"My cousin Pearl recently exchanged letters with a company that places mail order brides with men out west."

"A mail order bride? I'd be leaving one untenable situation for another."

"That's the beauty of this particular matching service," Emmaline explained. "You don't have to make a match until you meet the person up front. At the moment, they're looking for woman who are willing to marry and take part in the next Oklahoma

Land Run in April."

"Land run? You mean where they race across barren countryside in search of a spot to homestead?"

Emmaline nodded vigorously, obviously caught up in her own suggestion. "It's all so romantic, if you think about it. Going into the unknown with a man you've just met and married." Helping Lily out of her petticoats, Emmaline reminded her, "You're the one who's always saying how you crave adventure, rather than a mundane life as a Boston socialite. Now's your chance. Assuming you really meant what you said."

Lily settled herself in at her dressing table and handed Emmaline her hairbrush. Closing her eyes, she let the rhythm of the soft bristles being drawn through her long red tresses relax her.

After a few moments, she asked, "Exactly what would I have to do to get in on this grand adventure."

"From what I remember in the flyer Pearl received, you send in your name and particulars like height and weight, a photograph, and answer some questions about health. They even have a spot on the form for you to write down you'd want in a husband. It's almost as if you'd be looking for a mail order groom."

A mail order groom? Lily held up her hand and touched the tip of one finger with her thumb. "He'd

have to be a Christian, of course." Ticking off the
next finger, she continued. "He should be my age or
a few years older, but not *old* old."

"A hard worker would be good," Emmaline said,
her suggestion causing Lily to tap a third finger.

"He has to have a vision for his... our... future.
Not just someone who wants to grab a plot of land
with no idea what to do with it."

Giggling, Emmaline, added, "Handsome and tall
with big hands."

"Big hands?"

A second giggle escaped, but Emmaline tamped
it down. "Never mind. It's not important."

Lily wasn't so sure. Something about the man
having 'big hands' had certainly set off Emmaline's
girlish side.

"How do I get the application?" Lily asked.
Surely it wouldn't hurt to have a look.

"I'll see if Pearl has a spare. I know they sent her
a few, no doubt hoping she has friends who might be
interested."

"I'm not saying I'm going to fill it out, of course,
but it would be interesting to take a peek at what
they're offering."

"Exactly," Emmaline agreed. Setting the brush
aside, she stepped back and reached for Lily's
nightdress. "Let's get you out of that corset and into
bed before your parents get home. I can tell them
you retired early with a headache. That way, you can

put off your mother's rant until morning."

"You're the sweetest, Emmaline. I truly hope your young man realizes how special you are and offers you a ring."

"One thing's for certain, Miss Lily, if I can get you squared away first—even if it means sending you off a train headed west—it'll make leaving my employ a whole lot easier."

Lily sank into the plush mattress of her huge, canopy bed, and drew the silky covers up to her chin. Yes, she had told Emmaline—and anyone else who would listen—that she craved adventure. If traveling by train to Wichita, meeting and marrying a perfect stranger, and setting out across barren land formerly belonging to one of the many Indian tribes was what it took to slake her thirst for excitement, then so be it.

She couldn't very well claim to want something so desperately and then be too cowardly to follow through.

Could she?

More Sweet/Clean/Inspirational Romance
From Nancy Fraser

Historical/Western Historical

Abigail

Runaway Brides of the West Series

Can she escape her father's plan to marry her off and make her own way in small-town Colorado?

Lily's Luck

Land Run Brides

Can a spoiled debutante and a would-be cattle rancher make their unusual marriage work amid the excitement of an Oklahoma Land Run?

Ella

Prairie Roses Collection #4

Will a widow's faith and determination allow her to trust again and make a safe home for her family, while welcoming the handsome marshal into her heart? Wagon train romance.

A Christmas Baby for Beatrice

Mail-Order Brides First Christmas Series

Can a well-educated horticulturist and a widow find the true happiness they both deserve in the wilds of Washington State's pine forest? Mail-order bride romance.

An Honorable Man for Katarina

Multi Award-Winning Romance

Can a woman held against her will for six years make a new life for herself and her children with the help of the local sheriff?

Erin's Peachy-Keen Christmas

Roaring Twenties Romance

Can a young woman displaced because of her party-going friends find a new purpose with the widowed solicitor and his young son?

Seth's Secretive Bride

Matchmaker's Mix-Up Series

She's looking for a professional man in California. He wants a mature woman to help with his emotionally-challenged son. What they get is each other.

Contemporary

Harvest Hearts

Pumpkin Patch Romance Series
Can the widowed mystery writer caring for her grandmother with dementia find happiness with a retired navy seal who's inherited his uncle's farm? A Later-in-Life Romance about old friends reunited by circumstance.

Mitch

Last Man Standing Series
Will the architect be able to ignore the newly hired, and very beautiful, project manager and remain single? Or, is he about to relinquish his position as 'last man standing'.

Escape to Paradise

A Vacation Romance Series
Will the ex-military man and corporate attorney known as 'Viper' find what they're both looking for on the beautiful island paradise of Grand Cayman Island? Or, will they be risking far more than just their hearts?

Avocado Toast
Orchard Brides Series
Will Chloe's faith and determination help her lead
Drew through his difficult decisions and bring them
what they both need... a love that transcends their
everyday challenges.

Once Upon an Angel
Novice angel-in-training, Ariel Pearce, needs to earn
her wings. Will taking the newcomer along on her
next assignment be just what she needs to succeed?
A heartfelt double couple romance with a touch of
fantasy!

Christmas Carole
Can a single mom of two turn the holiday grinch
into a believer? Or, will it take the magic of the 'wish
stick' to bring two opposites together in time for a
perfect holiday?

*All of Nancy's Sweet/Inspirational books are
available on Kindle Unlimited.*

Still to Come in 2022

Holly Berry Inn
Christmas at the Inn Series
Contemporary ~ December 9th

A Christmas Grinch for Anya
Dickens Holiday Romance Collection
Contemporary ~ December 12th

Audrey
Christmas Quilt Brides Series
Historical Western ~ December 16th

Meet Author Nancy Fraser

Nancy Fraser a Top 100 best-selling and award-winning author.

She's also the granddaughter of a Methodist minister known for his fire-and-brimstone approach to his faith. Nancy has brought some of his spirit into her Christian romances. And, her own off-beat sense of humor to her clean & wholesome books.

When not writing (which is almost never), Nancy dotes on her five wonderful grandchildren and looks forward to traveling and reading when time permits. Nancy lives in Atlantic Canada where she enjoys the relaxed pace and colorful people.

9 798360 943150